Deadly Ghost

ANGUS BRODIE AND MIKAELA FORSYTHE MURDER MYSTERY
MYSTERY
BOOK TWELVE

CARLA SIMPSON

OLIVERHEBERBOOKS

Cover art by Dar Albert at Wicked Smart Designs

Published by Oliver-Heber Books

0 9 8 7 6 5 4 3 2 1

Ghosts of the past...

Prologue

SHE CLOSED the door to the library, and prying eyes.

"It is time for your morning tea, Mamà."

The woman in the chair smiled faintly.

"So many years, and now you are here," she said. Her hand shook slightly as she accepted the cup of tea.

"We are together now and I will be stronger soon, with your care."

So many years, the younger woman thought. So many secrets, so many lies—more than twenty years of them as something hardened inside her.

The letters had revealed the truth of the life she should have had. She forced the smile to her lips.

"Be sure to drink all of your tea, Mamà."

She wore a black gown, appropriate to the occasion, her hair tucked beneath a black hat, features hidden behind a veil that would have revealed something other than grief.

The servants had all been dismissed, except for the house-keeper. The home she had always known was to be sold.

There would be little left after her mother's illness, the solicitor told her, as the vicar recited the litany for the dead over the open grave.

So very sad, yet enough to keep her for a short while. Yet she had prospects, the solicitor had suggested then. After all, she was educated. She might find a position as a lady's companion, or tutor. She might marry, all quite acceptable.

Proper and acceptable, for a young woman of her circumstances, from a well-placed family, and all utterly loathsome.

Family.

If it hadn't been so ridiculous, she would have laughed at the word.

Hadn't she questioned it from time to time? That feeling that she didn't quite *belong,* perhaps in the way that children thought of things that eventually went away.

It had not.

It was during that time only a handful of years earlier, while her mother was preoccupied—perhaps that was more appropriate than grief-stricken over Sir William's declining health, then mourning his death—that she had discovered those letters from over twenty years before.

Sir William—oddly she had always thought of him by his given name. Not *Father,* a man who was distant, indifferent to her, as if she didn't exist. As if he knew ...

Oh, he had provided for her—the tutors, the exclusive finishing school in Paris, an extended trip abroad, and then the past years living in France.

Everything, except a father's love.

There had been no confrontation with her mother over the letters that explained so much, hidden away like precious mementos. To be taken out from time to time and read over again and again for a lost love?

She had tucked them away where she had found them, something cold growing inside her.

Secrets and lies.

The vicar's words for the soul of a *'good and honorable woman'* whispered among the trees that seemed to weep over the headstones of nearby graves in the drizzling rain. And the man who was there in his common clothes, the stovepipe hat, scribbling in his little notebook.

Burke was the name. He wrote for the crime sheets in the daily newspapers— now it seemed reduced to writing about the dead.

More lies—about a prominent family, service to the Crown, and a life well lived. Yet, lies could be useful.

"Miss?"

She stiffened at the manner in which the vicar addressed her now, as the service ended.

Not Lady Grantham, as it should have been, for now. Still, the omission strengthened her and gave her purpose.

"If you should wish to remain?" he suggested, appropriately somber with his pious dignity.

A question, no doubt for the usual mourners he served, immersed in grief, who couldn't bear the loss of a loved one.

There was nothing for her here, certainly not sadness. She shook her head, sending the vicar on his way, then turned to the man beside her.

"*Il est temps,*" she told him in French. It was time.

WE HAD all been encamped at Old Lodge, my great aunt's estate in the north of Scotland, over the past several months, waiting out the influenza epidemic that had gripped London.

The wife of the estate manager, Mrs. Hutton, had provided her homemade remedy for the midges that made life intolerable in the warmer months. A concoction I knew well from my own childhood stayovers at Old Lodge, a mixture of peppermint oil and witch hazel, liberally applied. Very effective if one didn't mind the smell. We did not, in exchange for respite from the voracious, stinging insects.

Aunt Antonia had returned to Sussex Square with her household staff weeks earlier, as reports of influenza, all but gone from the city, had eventually reached us. After all, she had the forthcoming *holiday season* to prepare for, never at a loss for some rather unusual but always fascinating ideas for the Christmas celebration.

My sister and her husband James Warren, who also happened to be my publisher, had traveled first to Brighton for a brief stayover when the epidemic first occurred, then remained until the health crisis had passed.

They had returned to London the week before, after being assured that it was quite safe, particularly for my sister, Linnie, who they announced was expecting their first child. They hadn't lost any time on that one!

Linnie had been previously married, a disastrous affair that ended badly, and she had lost a child during that time. That loss had changed her. Always quite serious, gifted with her painting talents, she had withdrawn even further at the subsequent scandal from that first marriage.

We had traveled together to the South of France, then an earlier trip to Brighton with the hope of drawing her out once more. In time, she seemed to put that painful episode behind her. And now there was James Warren.

Intelligent, quite handsome, and with a sense of humor that often left us all in stitches, he had ignored my sister's resolve to live a solitary life with her paintings. He didn't give a fig about the past scandal and had persuaded her that he simply could not live without her.

He supported her return to her painting and refused to let her dwell on the past. Both were creative—her with artistic successes, James with his publishing endeavors. They were very much like two peas in a pod.

A child had been very much hoped for. I was enormously happy for both of them.

At Old Lodge, Lily, whom I had persuaded to come to London, had discovered a part of Scotland far different from the poor streets of Edinburgh where we first met. She was very near eighteen years of age now as near as she could guess, having been orphaned to the streets.

Her early life working as a lady's maid in a brothel had

imbued her with a certain mistrust of people. She was extremely intelligent, frequently cynical, inquisitive, and too often bold with a blunt sarcasm that appeared at the most unexpected moments. She reminded me much of myself.

The agreement for her to come to London had included education, a place to live, and an admittedly odd collection of *family* that included myself, my great aunt, my sister, most certainly Brodie, along with his companion in childhood crime, Munro, and of course James Warren.

"*That one will try yer patience, not to mention her lady-ship's,*" Brodie had commented about Lily when the arrangement was made.

Yet he had stepped in as a sort of surrogate 'uncle,' as it were. They did have a great deal in common, and he wasn't fooled by her schemes.

I wasn't concerned about my great aunt taking on the responsibility of another young person. She had survived raising both my sister and me. As unconventional as she was with her interests, early travels, and a family line that went back to William the Conqueror, she was thrilled at the idea of another young spirit at Sussex Square.

"*She must of course live here,*" she insisted at the time. "*It makes no sense for her to live at Mayfair, and certainly not the office on the Strand when you and Mr. Brodie are off on your inquiry cases. Here, we can plan our adventures together.*"

As I have said, it was a somewhat unusual arrangement, but Lily had thrived, with a few bruises, lectures, and boring tutors along the way.

As for Brodie ...

In addition to a successful private inquiry enterprise, he had acquired a family, if albeit an unconventional one, after losing his own early on as a child.

I had never intended to wed. After a previous engagement, my travels, and my sister's dreadful first experience, I had quite simply decided that expectation was not for myself. I was of the opinion that there was not a man I might consider living my life with.

The house at Mayfair with my housekeeper was quite enough. I could not envision running a household, throwing society parties, wiping children's runny noses, and patching up skinned knees, while said husband took himself off to his club for ... shall we say, other interests, such as gambling and ruining the family fortunes.

I did have vivid memories of those failings from my own childhood and was determined that I would not experience them in my own adult life.

Then, there was Brodie.

Not at all what society would have approved for me, with his inquiry business and previous work with the Metropolitan Police, not to mention a somewhat criminal past that raised its head from time to time.

And perhaps still? Most fascinating, I had to admit.

He had lived first on the streets of Edinburgh, where he learned to survive by his wits with his good friend Munro, and then on the streets of London. Not at all what was expected, least of all for myself.

And then there was that *other thing,* along with a colorful recommendation from my great aunt of all people.

"He is a man you can trust. He does exactly as he says, and gets the job done. And ..."

That other thing she had recommended highly—he made my toes curl in such a delicious, maddening way.

It might also have been the way he looked at me with that

dark gaze, the way he understood me, valued my opinions and thoughts.

Of course, there was also my determination, which he referred to as my 'blasted stubbornness.' As he was not hesitant to point out, that often took me in a direction I perhaps shouldn't go in our inquiry cases, in spite of his concerns.

There were other words that went along with that, in Scots, which I did not understand however needed no explanation.

Quite simply, how could I possibly *not* accept that simple marriage proposal at Old Lodge? I could not.

Brodie had been encamped with all of us at Old Lodge, and returned to London the week previous, while Lily and I had remained for several more days.

He had been immediately drawn into an inquiry case with the Agency. When I returned, he had simply explained that it was a routine inquiry case, possibly a matter of a philandering husband, although one of some high rank in Parliament.

That off-handed explanation was undoubtedly meant to avoid my protests—not for the first time—against working with Agency.

Not that Lily's and my return left us without anything to occupy ourselves.

My publisher and new brother-in-law, James Warren, had arranged a reception for me at Hatchards in Piccadilly upon the release of my latest *Emma Fortescue* novel.

The book series had come from my travels abroad and met with enormous success. It seemed that readers in London and beyond, mostly women I will admit, were quite enthusiastic about reading something that was not ancient literature.

James was convinced that it was not only due to the mystery in each one, but the adventures that seemed to appeal to a great many.

Lily and I had returned the day before quite late, and she had stayed over at the townhouse in Mayfair. She was to depart in a few days for Paris to enroll in the private finishing school my sister and I had both attended. To say that the dear girl was not particularly eager to be sent off was somewhat of an understatement.

She had been tutored in French for the past several months and had made great progress. That progress, I had discovered while at Old Lodge, included several colorful words that I had immediately recognized, forcing me to hold back my surprise and laughter all at once as tears rolled down my cheeks.

We had a conversation about proper etiquette and deportment at the time. She had looked at me with a wide-eyed innocence that reminded me that I had said far worse things in the past.

After breakfast provided by my housekeeper, Mrs. Ryan, we arrived in good time at Hatchards bookstore. There was a robust crowd inside the store with a line that had begun to form on the sidewalk beyond in spite of the cold chill of the morning.

Lily grinned at me as the excited buzz of conversations greeted us as we entered the store.

"The ladies of London seem to be fond of Emma Fortescue," she commented as a woman nearby, who appeared very near my great aunt's age, appeared to be somewhat overcome as she spoke with a companion.

"Emma is so daring, so brave, and the things she does. Have you read the previous book? You absolutely must purchase it as well. There is a man she has taken up with," she fanned herself in spite of the cold morning, as she leaned in closer to her companion. "It's rumored that he also appears in this latest novel. Sinful, absolutely sinful," she added with a smile. "It's rumored that the man is an acquaintance of the author."

Those rumors—acquaintance indeed.

I recognized the expression on Lily's face that could only be described as a smirk.

"It's good that Mr. Brodie doesna read your books," she commented.

Cheeky girl. Yet I could only imagine the protests that would cause.

"So good to see you!" James greeted us enthusiastically as we arrived at the desk in a small area at the back of the store. There, copies of my latest *Emma* book awaited those who hadn't already purchased one, while a tea service was arranged beside them.

"I considered that a bit of Old Lodge whisky might be preferrable but the manager is a very proper sort," he teased. "Yet, I wouldn't put it past him to take a nip once in a while."

I laughed. "Only one?"

"Or several," he suggested in a lowered tone, then added, "We do seem to have a tremendous response today to your new novel."

"It might be the character she introduced in her last book," Lily interjected with an expression of wide-eyed innocence.

"Ah, yes. Mr. MacKenzie," James replied. "Linnie mentioned something about that from the early draft you provided her. She was quite ... intrigued," he added with a smile.

I did remember her reaction several months earlier, as she read an early draft of the book.

"Good heavens, Mikaela! You simply cannot put that in

there!" she said at the time, as I had noticed the sudden color in her cheeks. *"However did you come by such a thing?"*

I replied that I had it on good advice from our great aunt. Linnie had been left quite speechless.

"Be that as it may, I can say that your 'publisher' is most appreciative," James commented. "The only issue might be having enough books to sell today. I will see to having more brought over from the warehouse."

And he set off to see it done.

"I will have a look about," Lily announced as the manager of the bookstore arrived and greeted me. "And see what other comments the ladies make."

As I said, cheeky girl.

Over the next several hours there were several questions from those who purchased the books:

Did the things I wrote about actually happen?

Was it exciting to travel the Continent?

Was it dangerous? Did I actually know that ancient art of self-defense?

And then a frequent comment:

I do hope that you will be writing about the gentleman again ...

Gentleman. Brodie would have been highly amused.

Lily returned frequently through the afternoon that followed, with her usual observations about the customers she observed while wandering about the book shop.

"That woman in the green gown just popped a button. One more and she will be completely undone."

That would make an interesting comment in the daily newspaper.

"The other one with her reminds me of a goat."

Which of course raised the question, when had she ever

seen a goat, since she'd lived in Edinburgh and now London, with occasional trips to Old Lodge?

"I've seen pictures!" she protested.

I was reminded that she would make a successful inquiry agent when she completed her education, beyond burst buttons and goats, of course, and in spite of Brodie's objections.

And then she was off once more. "I might even find a book to read."

I recommended Jane Austen or Mr. Dickens, and received what I referred to as the 'Lily look,' mouth twisted into a frown with a sideways glance for emphasis.

As the afternoon passed, the line of customers thinned. Mr. Holloway, the manager, was pleased, as his clerks had sold a good number of books.

"It is always a pleasure to have you visit us when you have a new book, Lady Forsythe," he had commented as another woman stepped from the line with a book in hand.

"The adventures are quite exciting," she commented. "I've never traveled outside London, and I do look forward to the book." Then the oft-heard comment of the day.

"Is *Mr. MacKenzie* in this one as well?"

I assured her that *he* was.

"Oh, marvelous," she replied with an excited smile.

I signed a half-dozen more books the manager had requested, as Lily returned from exploring the store, and café across the street, and other fascinations.

"Yer here!" she commented with obvious surprise as she returned, the Scots accent slipping through, as it had a way of doing when she was excited about something.

"As I have been most of the day," I replied the obvious as I put on my jacket, then gathered my travel bag with a copy of the book for my great aunt. She was quite a devotee of Emma Fortescue's adventures.

"It's just that ..." She frowned. "I thought I saw ye just there on the street, looking in the shop window ..." She indicated the front of the shop. "But when I looked again, you were gone. I thought ye might have stepped out for some air. This place is stuffy."

"I've been here the entire time," I informed her as I handed the clerk the additional books that I'd signed.

Lily's frown was still there in spite of my assurances. Having lived by her wits on her own, I had discovered—as had a series of tutors—that she had a keen mind and wasn't easily deceived. I didn't doubt that she had seen *someone*. I had also learned it was best not to argue a point with a stubborn Scot.

"I know what I saw," Lily insisted as we left the bookstore.

Two

"SHE WAS QUITE CERTAIN," I commented about Lily's encounter at the bookstore the day before as Brodie and I arrived at the office on the Strand.

He had returned late to the townhouse the previous evening, tired, with a deep frown that had not eased until after a bit of Old Lodge whisky and the late supper Mrs. Ryan had held over for him.

I had learned in the past not to ask my usual questions about the new inquiry case for the Agency. It was best to pick the appropriate moment—when the frown disappeared.

It was over breakfast this morning when he had finished a second cup of coffee that he set his cup down. He explained that the new case had to do with a member of Parliament who had been seen in unusual company. It raised the question that he might be participating in clandestine activities.

The company he was seen with might be a lover or mistress, or someone for an entirely different purpose. However, he was most clever about the relationship, and it would take some time to determine what it was about.

We had then discussed the events of my day on the ride to the office, including that encounter Lily had been so adamant about.

"You are to blame for her determination to pursue something," I informed him now.

That dark gaze narrowed. "How might that be?"

"You encourage her interest in our inquiry cases—*observe, make note of anything unusual, then investigate.*" I quoted what he had once told her about inquiry work.

He sat back in his chair at the desk, pipe in hand as he sent a stream of fragrant smoke that I liked very much into the air.

"And ye would send her off to finishing school in Paris instead," he replied. There had been more than one conversation about that.

"And what might she learn there?" he asked with another puff on that pipe.

I had to admit I agreed that it might *not* be time well spent. Lily didn't want to go to Paris. However, my great aunt thought it would be a great experience for her; she would meet other young people from other parts of Europe, study different languages, broaden her experience.

Recalling my own time there, the word *'experience'* had a variety of meanings for a young woman who was too bold for her own good.

I did realize that was a bit like the pot calling the kettle black, as Brodie had pointed out when the arrangements were made.

"Are you saying that you believe that it would be better for her here, in London?" I had replied.

In that maddening way he had, he didn't reply, but just looked at me. It did seem as if I had answered my own question.

"Perhaps six months, not a full year," I suggested. Never let it be said that I wasn't capable of compromising.

"Perhaps, if the place is still standing."

The truth was that I highly suspected any learning experience would be the other way round. I had visions of Lily entertaining her fellow students with bawdy renditions of songs and stories learned in that brothel in Edinburgh.

The truth also was, I'd been having that argument with myself the past several weeks.

Six months, I thought. Then she could return and …

That was the question. I knew quite well where her thoughts lay in that regard.

Brodie had gone over the details of the new inquiry case that the Agency had been asked to take in consideration of sensitivity regarding Sir Charles Talmadge, the member of Parliament who was under suspicion.

He had made cursory inquiries when an unexpected piece of information had come to light regarding Lady Talmadge, who was considerably younger than her husband and had been born in Budapest.

It seemed that she had a penchant for older, powerful men after a rumored series of lovers. According to additional information she frequently attended the women's exercises classes at the German Gymnasium.

"Ye have gone there in the past," Brodie pointed out. "And yer well acquainted with Herr Schmidt …"

I knew where he was leading with this. His inquiries might draw suspicion, particularly if Lady Talmadge happened to be present.

I had frequently attended the gymnasium in the past, and it was unlikely that I would draw attention.

It seemed that Lady Talmadge kept regular appointments

in the afternoon, five days a week, which did seem a bit extreme.

My recent attendance had been to sharpen my skills with the rapier—no pun intended—as Lily had become quite proficient with the blade in her scrimmaging about in the Sword Room at Sussex Square. The present instructor, Herr Renner, was highly skilled; however he wasn't available until later, which should be perfect for encountering Lady Talmadge if she followed her usual schedule.

I passed the time until then by making a list on the chalkboard, recording information that Brodie had learned so far in the investigation.

"How old is Lady Talmadge?" I asked as I finished making those notes.

"Somewhere very near yer own age, I would suppose."

"You've seen her?"

"Hmmm," he remarked, which was no remark at all as he made notes in the small notebook he always carried, a habit from his days as an inspector with the MET.

"And Sir Talmadge must be very near seventy years, the last time I saw him," I added.

No comment this time.

"It doesn't seem as if he married her to sit before the fire, holding hands in his dotage, and fifty years difference does make one wonder if he is ..."

That dark gaze met mine with an amused expression.

"Capable," I finished the thought.

"And ye would have some experience with that?" Brodie inquired, as he took another draw from the pipe.

"You are somewhat older," I pointed out.

"Is that a complaint, Mikaela Forsythe Brodie?"

"Not at all, Mr. Brodie," I replied and turned back to the

board and added my final thoughts to the list—*Age Difference —potential lovers?*

After the months of inactivity as far as our inquiry cases were concerned, it was good to be off pursuing information and possible clues. And it was an opportunity for me to polish my skills with the blade, at the same time I might be able to learn something about Lady Talmadge that might be useful in the Agency's inquiry case.

As far as I was concerned, the sooner Brodie was finished with it, the better. Not that I had anything against the Agency or Sir Avery, other than Brodie being almost killed in a previous case.

The German Gymnasium was in Camden in the north end of London at St. Pancras Street.

It was located in a two-story brick building built several decades earlier by the German community in London. It was well-known, and I had taken lessons there after discovering my great aunt's sword collection at Sussex Square. Admittedly, a rapier was far different from a broad sword, I quickly learned, perfecting the movements that made a rapier so deadly.

I had then studied further on one of my travels and learned the ways of the deadly Khopesh, an Egyptian curved sword with a sickle-shaped blade. I discovered that it was far superior in many ways when it came to handling a sword. And, as I was reminded in a recent case, extremely lethal.

More than once my great aunt had expressed misgivings when it came to telling me about our ancestors—a somewhat fierce lot, who first arrived on English soil from France eight hundred years earlier—after I had sneaked into the Sword Room at Sussex Square.

I was nine years old at the time and quite fascinated, though hardly able to wield the huge swords that were there. At least not yet.

The fascination was still there years later when my sister and I were sent to private school France.

There, I trained with a fencing master. Of course, a rapier is quite different from a broadsword, however the basics are quite the same. And that training did allow for me to avoid some of the more boring classes of private school.

Brodie accompanied me on the ride to the gymnasium and had the driver stop at the street across.

"Are there any particular instructions?" I asked. There usually were.

"Aye. Best not to approach Lady Talmadge, it might draw suspicion if she has some involvement in this," he replied in that same circumspect manner.

"Make note of any interactions she might have with anyone, and get the name of anyone she interacts with from the person at the front desk."

His hand closed over mine. There was obviously more.

"Dinna draw attention to yerself since we dinna know yet how the woman might be involved."

Of course, dear, I thought but didn't say it. It wasn't as if I hadn't done this very same thing several times in the past.

"Do you want me to follow her when she leaves?" I suggested. "It could be useful."

He shook his head. "This is only to observe persons she might be in contact with. The gymnasium would be the perfect opportunity. That will be enough fer now."

He assisted me down from the cab, then handed me the

bag that held my walking skirt, a garment that allowed movement about the gymnasium floor, a fitted blouse, and the padded leather vest Aunt Antonia had made for me when I insisted on taking up the sport, along with long leather gloves.

"I'll not have you returning minus a hand and bleeding all over the place," she had remarked at the time. *"I cannot understand where you get such ideas or your fascination with the sport."*

As they say, the apple had not fallen far from the tree.

"Ye are to observe, not follow," Brodie repeated. "There are enough drivers here about during the day when ye leave afterward."

I caught the frown. "I will be quite safe, and I do have the revolver."

"Aye."

He waited with his driver as I set off toward the gymnasium with a detailed description he had provided earlier of Lady Talmadge.

Upon entering the gymnasium, I signed in at the desk. A large, stout woman I would not have wanted to meet in a dark alley introduced herself as Gerta and asked my name.

"Are you joining the ladies' exercise group? They're about to begin their morning session."

"I will be joining Monsieur Bertrand this morning," I replied.

"The fencing instructor?" She was somewhat taken aback.

I nodded. "I made an appointment earlier."

She checked the log book, then muttered an acknowledgment.

"It will be near the boxing ring," she informed me.

Which was across from the fencing floor, I noted, and would provide a prime location for watching the ladies who had begun to gather for their class from the fencing *piste.*

I thanked her and crossed the floor toward the dressing room. It gave me the opportunity to glance among the ladies as they prepared to begin their morning exercises. I caught sight of a young woman in the second row who matched the description Brodie had provided.

She was full-figured, pretty, with thick blonde hair gathered back from her face, and high cheekbones. I made note of the color of her costume—magenta with black trim—so that I would be able to easily observe her when I returned to the floor.

I quicky changed, then left the dressing rooms and joined Monsieur Bertrand at the *piste*. He bowed in acknowledgement.

"I thought there must be some mistake when I saw your name this morning, Lady Forsythe. I am intrigued that it is not a mistake."

"I have visited several times."

"You are familiar with the rapier?"

I nodded. "It has been some time, and I hoped to improve my skill."

He appeared to be quite amused.

"You would do well to take care with this one, Bertrand."

I recognized that deep baritone accent as Herr Schmidt crossed the floor and joined us.

"She is known to show no mercy. To myself included."

He was exaggerating, of course, yet I made no attempt to correct him.

"I am grateful that you could accommodate me on such short notice," I told Herr Schmidt. "I will have the need of one of your rapiers, as I did not bring my own."

"Of course," he replied and made a gesture toward the stand that contained several different dueling blades.

I selected one I was most familiar with, that also contained a tip blunted with cork.

"As I said, monsieur," he repeated. "Be careful. She is most skillful." He nodded curtly, then departed.

"You are familiar with how to proceed?" Monsieur Bertrand inquired.

I replied that I did as I donned the *epee* mask, then checked the weight of the rapier and assumed the *appropriate* stance on the floor as the ladies across the way moved into their next set of exercises.

Monsieur Bertrand was quite skillful, yet I sensed that he took great care with each parry and thrust so as not to overwhelm me. Even though it had been some time since I had made the basic moves, I found my counter-moves quickly returned. Our moves about the floor provided the opportunity to observe the ladies on the exercise floor, Lady Talmadge in particular.

Shift, deflect, attack. Then shift again, parry, as I pushed off my right leg, lunged and made contact with monsieur's shoulder, well-padded by his vest.

He acknowledged the contact and took a step back as I glanced across to the group of ladies as they finished one exercise series and took a moment to catch their breath, speaking with one another before beginning again.

The next point was his. I circled, then lunged and took the next point. He nodded, and we began again.

It was very near the noon when the ladies finished their exercises, and began to gradually make their way toward the dressing rooms while chatting amongst themselves.

I took a step back and raised the rapier in a salute, the usual signal that I yielded the floor. Monsieur Bertrand also took a step back and acknowledged the end of our training session.

"My compliments, Lady Forsythe. A most pleasurable encounter. You must return so that we may take up our next bout."

"And you as well, monsieur." I returned the rapier to the stand, then made my way to the ladies' dressing room.

The sound of conversations and laughter greeted me as I stepped into the room with the lockers where the women changed out of their exercise costumes.

I took a small towel from the stack on a table, then deliberately took a great deal of time as I wiped the dampness from my face and neck.

"I have never seen a woman handle a sword."

The comment came from a woman who had been part of the exercise class.

"Have you ever been injured?"

I turned and handed her one of the towels from the table. "A few close encounters, but nothing serious."

I used those moments of conversation to change my clothes as I watched Lady Talmadge change into a dark green gown and jacket.

There was no conversation between her and any of the other ladies, yet I did see a small piece of paper she removed from the pocket of her jacket as she turned to leave.

"My husband wouldn't approve," the woman commented as I grabbed my bag and turned to follow others who were leaving, including Lady Talmadge. "But maybe I could take lessons."

It did seem as if I might have created more business for Monsieur Bertrand.

I quickly left the dressing room and followed the ladies as some chatted while others moved purposefully toward the entrance of the gymnasium with Lady Talmadge among them.

Others followed as we stepped out on the street, and crowded the sidewalk to find a cab as a light rain set in. A private coach rounded the corner as the other ladies began to depart afoot in several directions.

It was only a glimpse and it was quickly done, as one of the older women brushed up against Lady Talmadge. She begged pardon as Lady Talmadge reached out, that slip of paper quickly passed between them.

I made a mental note of the woman to whom Lady Talmadge had passed that note. She was dressed in a dark blue gown of considerable quality and a black coat, her hat pulled low over dark hair, the brim not quite shielding her face from the rain.

There was only a brief acknowledgment from Lady Talmadge, then she stepped from the curb and entered the private coach that had arrived.

Lady Talmadge stepped up into the coach.

My first instinct was to follow one of them, and none the wiser unless they might have been looking for it as I had. But what of the other woman? Who was she and what was on that piece of paper Lady Talmadge had passed to her?

My efforts to obtain a driver were unsuccessful at the moment with the other ladies scrambling aboard the cabs and hacks available to get out of the rain. I could only watch the direction the other woman had departed.

I returned to the gymnasium to speak with Gerta at the front desk, and described the woman I had seen Lady Talmadge pass that note to.

"I thought that I recognized her, an old friend from school," I invented as I went along. "If you might have her name, or where I might reach her. It would be so good to catch up with each other."

I will admit that Gerta looked at me as if I might have taken a step away from sanity, yet with a grumble she scanned down the list of names for the morning class.

"Doesn't your conscience bother you?" Linnie had asked, after the inquiry case when she had been abducted, and there had been more than one small lie to find her location

"Not when lives are at stake," I had replied. That had ended the conversation.

As far as I was concerned, the end justified the means, something I had learned from Brodie in the course of that first inquiry case.

"I may have led ye astray," he had commented over one of my more creative endeavors. *"And a lady at that. Are ye ashamed of yerself?"*

I assured had him that I wasn't.

The truth was that I didn't care where he *led me* as long as we were together. And that had led to some very interesting encounters.

Gerta had found the woman's name. "She has been here a few times. Miss M. Holcomb."

"Of course ..." I replied. "Of Milford Square in Sussex," I replied with absolutely no idea where she was from, but it accomplished what I was after.

"Not Sussex," she replied in that thick accent. "Waverly, according to the address when she signed for the class. She receives the bill and pays on time. No trouble."

'Miss M. Holcomb of Waverly Place,' if that was her real name, who had received that note from Lady Talmadge.

I thanked Gerta, then gathered my bag to leave.

The last of the women and several men who had finished their exercise session had clustered under the awning at the sidewalk as they waited for drivers to arrive.

They were a mixed group—some of the women wearing the costume of a housekeeper or seamstress as they took time away from their work to attend the gymnasium, the men wearing wool day coats over trousers, mostly German spoken among them.

As other drivers arrived and passengers crowded round, a young woman stepped from among them and quickly crossed the street as a private coach arrived. I might have paid no attention if she hadn't looked back.

She was slender and wore a long coat in a deep shade of gray, with a black ship-boat hat over dark auburn hair tucked under.

It was not her clothes that caught my attention, nor the fact that she appeared a great deal younger than the other ladies of the exercise class who crowded the sidewalk in the pouring rain, as she ran toward a coach that waited.

She hesitated, then looked back over her shoulder, her gaze briefly meeting mine. In that moment, it was very much like looking into a mirror.

I started across the street, but the coach was already pulling away from the curb, and quickly disappeared into the traffic of cabs, carts, and hacks that filled the street.

Three

"I KNOW WHAT I SAW," I told Brodie over supper that evening, after providing him the information about Lady Talmadge and her encounter with the woman by the name of M. Holcomb of Waverly Place, London.

Then, over a dram of whisky afterward in the front parlor at the townhouse, I shared that most unusual encounter with the young woman outside the gymnasium.

"There are many persons with red hair," he commented. "Although not as appealing as yer own, particularly when ye wear it down ..."

There was that smile as he refilled his glass. I shook my head when he offered to refill my own.

"It wasn't just the color of her hair. It was very much like seeing ... my reflection in a mirror. Oh, not exactly the same but near enough that it was most curious. And the way she looked at me, for just a moment before getting into the coach. It was as if ..."

"As if wot ...?"

"Familiarity," I replied. I didn't know how else to describe it. "As if I should know her."

There was more. I went on to describe Lily's encounter outside Hatchards bookstore. "She was quite adamant about the resemblance. She went on and on in great detail. You know how she can be about things."

"Aye, like a dog with a bone."

I ignored that comment.

"I suppose it could be nothing more than coincidence. Many cultures have myths and superstitions about such things, and believe that we all have a twin somewhere."

"A twin?" Brodie commented with some amusement.

"Two people identical to each other," I explained. "There are occasionally twins born from time to time that one hears of."

"I know what it means. I'm not certain the world is ready for two of ye."

He went to the fireplace and added more coal against the evening chill that had set in in the past few weeks.

"It is possible the young woman had business nearby," Brodie suggested. "And it was a matter of simply returning to her coach as the weather set in."

He was right of course. Camden was a working-class part of London with factories, markets, work-shops, and the gymnasium, crowded with carts and wagons on any given day.

It could be nothing more than a random encounter. As for the similarity of appearance ...

The insistent sound of the telephone in the hallway pulled me from that thought. It eventually ceased.

It was not unusual to receive a telephone call at the town-house, most usually when Brodie had already left the office on the Strand and some matter arose that needed his attention regarding a case we were working on.

Mrs. Ryan appeared at the entrance to the parlor and announced the call was for me. It was my great aunt. I looked at Brodie with some surprise.

Not that it was all that unusual for her to call. She had become quite use to the 'demmed rude thing,' as she called the telephone that had been installed at Sussex Square.

"Here you are, dear," she replied when I picked up the hand-set. "I know this is short of notice, but there is a situation that has arisen and I need for you and Mr. Brodie to come to Sussex Square in the morning. I have also asked Lenore and Mr. Warren to join us. Ten o'clock, if you please. It is a most serious matter."

Ten o'clock in the morning?

It wasn't the time that was unusual, she was in the habit of rising quite early including our recent stay over at Old Lodge. It was something in her voice.

"Mikaela, dear."

Not a request but that insistence again at her voice. She was not one to insist on something.

"Yes, of course," I finally replied, even though I hadn't had the chance to speak with Brodie.

"Wot is it?" Brodie asked as I slowly returned to the parlor, going back over that conversation ... except it wasn't a conversation at all.

"Aunt Antonia has asked for us to meet with her at Sussex Square in the morning. She's also asked for Linnie and James to be there."

I spent a restless night following that telephone call from my great aunt.

My first thought was that she might have been taken ill. At her age it was to be expected, except there had been no indication in that conversation. She had been clear and succinct, even if a bit abrupt. And the simple truth was that if it was a health issue, her staff would call her physician, and then both Linnie and I would be made aware.

"It might be nothing more than some matter about her will and the estate. She mentioned it while we were at Old Lodge. I know little about such things, but knowin' her ladyship, she will want to make certain that everything is as it should be for ye and yer sister."

That did seem reasonable, and not so very long after she had spoken of it. I had paid little attention at the time as I was not preoccupied with it. And the truth was that I didn't want to think about the time when my great aunt would no longer be here.

After the dreadful loss of both our parents, she had been our family, the one who put back together the pieces of our lives. Yet, I knew it was important to her that everything be in order.

Yes, I thought, undoubtedly that is what this was about, as our driver turned into the entrance at Sussex Square.

It appeared that James and Linnie had already arrived by the coach that was already there, along with a second one.

I exchanged a look with Brodie as we climbed the steps to the entrance and were greeted by Mr. Symons, my great aunt's head butler.

"Good morning, Miss Mikaela, Mr. Brodie."

Brodie nodded his greeting as he handed over his coat and neck scarf.

"Mr. Symons..." I started to ask, and felt Brodie's reassuring hand on my arm.

"Beg your pardon, miss. Her ladyship has asked that everyone meet in the library upon arrival."

He had been with my great aunt for over thirty years, well before she brought Linnie and me to live at Sussex Square.

He had seen us—mostly myself—through our early adventures that would have seemed too much responsibility for a woman of our great aunt's station in life, not to mention her age at the time, to undertake.

But we had all somehow *muddled through,* as he once described it, and survived.

I handed over my umbrella and coat, attempting now to learn something from that stoic gaze.

"Is my great aunt well?"

"Yes, miss. Quite well."

That at least eliminated any illness or malady that might have necessitated the meeting on such short notice.

She rose from the settee as we arrived in the library. Linnie and James were seated nearby, with Lily beside them. Two more chairs sat across from them before the hearth.

I was somewhat surprised to see Sir Laughton, my great aunt's attorney, at the desk. That explained the additional coach as we arrived. I took one of the chairs, while Brodie chose to stand.

"We can now begin," Aunt Antonia announced.

"I have asked you here this morning because of a matter of grave importance that has made itself known that may affect all of you."

I had seen my great aunt in many situations, always in control, always with that same bearing and manner, something I had once described much like a field commander in spite of her eccentricities. This was no different, as she nodded to Sir Laughton then sat once more.

"If you please, Cedric."

"Yes, of course," he replied with a faint smile that was quickly gone as he stood.

"The matter which Lady Montgomery has spoken of and requested you to be here is of a delicate nature that has the potential to affect all of you."

He looked at me, then Linnie, and continued.

"She has received contact from a young woman who has made the claim that the late John Forsythe was her father." He indicated a letter before him on the desk, along with several papers and a small bundle of envelopes.

"The young woman has provided letters between Sir John and her late mother that appear to support her claim, as well as other documents."

I shifted uncomfortably as he continued. Our father's infidelities were well known. It was very much like an old wound that was being pried open once more, and I felt Brodie's hand on my shoulder.

"Who is she?" Linnie was the first to speak.

"Her name is Victoria Grantham," Sir Laughton replied. "Her mother was Lady Anne Grantham."

I noticed the look that passed between Sir Laughton and my great aunt, then he continued.

"According to the information provided by her representative, she had been living in France until several months ago. She became aware of the letters and documents upon her return, and Lady Grantham's passing."

It felt as if the walls of the library were closing in. I suddenly stood, unable to calmly sit there any longer as he continued to explain that my aunt had received the letter from the woman the day before, along with a packet of those other letters and documents.

All of the emotions that I had buried long ago were there once more as I thought of the last several days—the woman Lily had seen outside the bookstore, the woman I had seen in Camden the day before. That striking resemblance.

Both encounters a coincidence?

It hardly seemed so with what we were now being told as those memories clawed their way to the surface.

"Who is this representative?" I demanded, fighting back the anger that still came too easily.

"A solicitor by the name of Jerrod Handley," Sir Laughton replied.

"Do you know him?"

He gestured to the embossed letter that lay open on the desk.

"Not directly, however he is with Whitcomb and Handby Solicitors, a reputable firm here in London."

"What does she want?" I asked, somewhat sharply and caught my sister's startled expression at my bluntness.

"According to the letter received with these other letters and the documents, she wants only to know her real family."

I caught the look my great aunt gave me when I would have said what I wanted to say.

"I am available," Sir Laughton added. "If there should be questions, or you wish to respond to the letter."

Aunt Antonia stood then. "Thank you, Ceddy. As always."

"I will leave these with you." He laid that letter from the woman's representative on the desk along with the folded document and that wrapped bundle of old letters.

Linnie was the first to break the awkward silence after he

had left. "I suppose the thing to do would be to arrange a meeting."

"And she has now appeared after all these years? That is quite astounding," James commented.

He had only recently become a part of the family. I had no way of knowing what my sister might have shared with him about our childhood. She had been a good deal younger at that time, and I had shielded her from so many things. Admittedly, her memories were different from mine.

It was not the same for Brodie. He had experienced a great deal of loss as a child, forced to live on the streets after his mother's death, then in his time with the MET and during our private inquiry cases. One case in particular that had been difficult for both of us—homeless children rounded up and used for sport. The cruelty of it had opened those old wounds.

Still, it was then that I had shared the memories of that earlier tragedy, the horror and pain of it, the infidelities that were whispered about that he understood so very well. It had broken down the wall I had always kept around my feelings. And he was there. Just as he was now, his hand on my shoulder in quiet understanding.

He said nothing now. It wasn't necessary.

"I do believe an effort should be made to meet with her. You know as well as I, that it is very possible that her claim is legitimate," Linnie added. "We should at least be willing to consider the possibility."

"You may do as you wish," I replied. I was not convinced of the woman's claim, in spite of the letters and documents she had provided.

"But if she has documents to prove this ..." Linnie continued.

"In due time," Aunt Antonia interceded. "I will speak with

Sir Laughton again on the matter. Mikaela, Brodie, do remain."

"Yes, of course," James replied, as the family meeting was obviously at an end. "I do need to return to the office."

Linnie paused as they prepared to leave. "It must be very difficult for this Victoria Grantham as well," she reasoned. "I do hope that you will at least consider meeting with her."

Linnie had always been the one to make peace between us, our temperaments quite different—hers calm and reasonable, mine ... somewhat *different,* as Brodie would say.

"There are a great many questions still to be answered," I replied, not wanting to upset her in her condition. She squeezed my hand, then paused.

"There is the reception tomorrow evening at the gallery. With this upsetting news, I suppose we might cancel," she suggested.

"Not at all," Aunt Antonia informed her. "It is important for you. We shall be there to support you."

Much like the field commander, I thought. She waited until they had gone.

"With what has now happened, there are things you should know."

She sat once more, then indicated the side table with a decanter and glasses. "Mr. Brodie, if you please. It might be a bit early in the day—however I believe we might all do with a dram."

He poured three tumblers, then handed one to each of us.

"It is a very fine whisky," my great aunt said, looking quite thoughtfully into the glass. She drained the tumbler, then set it on the table beside her chair.

"I must go as well," Brodie said.

This was far different than James choosing to leave. This

was an understanding of the bond between me and my great aunt, things shared in the past, and apparently more to be shared now.

"I will see ye afterward." His hand gently brushed mine.

I nodded.

Lily followed him to the entrance of the library.

"I'll be in the sword room," she announced with a look at me, then at Aunt Antonia. And then we were alone.

"Another dram, Mikaela, if you please."

It was long into the afternoon when Aunt Antonia rose from her chair and set aside her empty tumbler. Lunch had been brought to the library, but I had no appetite.

We had spoken of many things—the woman's claim, the documents she had provided, along with those old letters. Yet the most stunning part of it—that my mother had known of the affair.

"I do not know when your mother first learned of it. Then the loss of the child she hoped for, and the illness that came afterward. I believe her malaise may have been caused by that loss and ... other things.

"She asked me to call on her at Pembrook after she became ill," my great aunt continued after asking me to pour her another dram of whisky.

"She knew about the gambling and the debts, and she was dreadfully concerned for you and Lenore. Though the family connection was somewhat distant, I assured her that she need have no worry in that regard."

Aunt Antonia smiled then and leaned over to pat my hand.

"We have had such an adventure, wouldn't you say, my dear? I would not have missed it for all the gold in the treasury." She drained the last of the whisky and set it on the table. "I do believe that Mr. Brodie is quite right. You and I are very much alike, my dear."

There was more that went unspoken in the look she gave me. She stood then.

"I will have Mr. Hastings bring 'round the coach. It does seem that the weather has turned quite dreadful," she said as she went to the entrance of the library, then paused.

"I believe that I will join Lily in the sword room for a go. I do hope the dear girl hasn't shredded the damask drapes." Another faint smile. "Such an adventure."

Very much alike, indeed, I thought, as I called for my coat and umbrella.

Mr. Hastings nodded in greeting as he held open the door of the coach when I left the manor.

"Mayfair, miss?"

"The Strand," I replied. "And slowly, please."

I needed time to think about everything my great aunt had told me, things I hadn't known as a child. As she said, it would have served no purpose.

It might have been an hour later, or perhaps two, when the coach finally stopped. I paid no attention on the ride from Sussex Square. I now peered out the glass at the familiar lights of the Strand.

Mr. Cavendish rolled out from the alcove on his platform as Mr. Hastings tipped his cap, then returned to his seat atop the coach and departed.

"The hound has been there all evenin', waiting for you." Mr. Cavendish pointed to the corner just beyond the smoke shop as Rupert came bounding toward us. "Wouldn't touch the meat pie I brought over from the Public House. Now I'll have to see if they have anything left for me own supper," he grumbled as I scratched Rupert behind the ears in greeting.

They set off together as I turned toward the steps that led to the office. I was certain that Miss Effie would be able to provide something for the hound.

Brodie looked up as I entered the office. He sat at the desk, the small note pad that he always carried before him.

"I thought ye might have decided to stay over at Sussex Square," he commented as that dark gaze fastened on me.

There were questions there, but he didn't ask in that way that he sensed my need to think things through for myself.

"There's supper on the stove," he said then and gestured to the ceramic plate rimmed with roses that my great aunt had provided to replace the tin one he used in the past.

"Mr. Cavendish brought it for ye earlier."

I wasn't hungry. It might have been the whisky, or the lunch my great aunt provided as we sat and spoke of things I had not known. But I had eaten very little.

I was suddenly bone-tired, as I once heard it described. I had wondered at the time what that meant. Now I knew.

"Mrs. Ryan?"

I had not thought to call her earlier to inform her that we would not be returning that night.

"I let her know that we would be staying here for the night."

I nodded. "I would like very much to go to bed now."

He took my umbrella from my icy hands, then unbuttoned my long coat and hung it on the stand.

I undressed in the room next to the office that had been turned into a bedroom for those occasions when we worked late, then crawled beneath the blanket in my slip and camisole.

He pulled the comforter up and tucked it around me.

"I have some notes to make about the case for the Agency," he said, and would have returned to the adjacent office.

I reached for his hand.

"Don't go."

The edge of the bed dipped under his weight. There was the sound of his boots as he removed them, then his solid warmth as he pulled me against him.

"Are ye all right?" he whispered.

"I will be."

Four

I SHARED everything with Brodie that my great aunt had told me—the things that would have served no purpose telling two young children at the time, suddenly orphaned after the deaths of both parents.

"What of yer sister?" Brodie asked. "Ye have to think of her as well."

"I am thinking of her," I replied over very strong coffee and breakfast at the Public House.

Most particularly of her longing for a family of her own after difficult things in the past.

"What will ye do then?" he asked as we returned to the office with a carton of food for Mr. Cavendish and Rupert.

"I want to read the letters."

Knowing me and my need to understand so very well, he simply nodded.

"There are things I must see to at the Agency."

The Talmadge inquiry. I understood that, as well.

He had Mr. Cavendish call for a cab. The service bell rang to let us know that a driver had arrived.

His hand closed around mine. He stared down at that simple bronze band he had given me, his thumb brushing the metal, warm from my hand.

"Whatever ye decide ..."

It was that simple—whatever I decided, that was to be done. Not in so many words, of course, but just in that simple gesture.

I pressed my hand against his cheek.

"Brodie ..."

His other hand closed around mine. He turned it in his, then pressed a kiss to the palm. My fingers curled as if to hold onto it.

"I know, lass."

I didn't immediately take out the letters after he left. I needed to gather my thoughts first, to set my emotions aside, as Brodie had once told me in that difficult case.

It was sometime later and more than one cup of coffee when I finally took them out of my bag and spread them on the top of the desk, along with those documents. And then began ...

20 April 18

Dear Anne,

So many thoughts, so many feelings. You must understand that I struggle with all of them.

The encounter in the park was unexpected,

and at the same time left me feeling something I have not felt in a very long time. A lightness of feeling to be certain, and your smile …

I look forward to seeing you again, if you should find yourself in the park.

John Forsythe

I sat back in my chair at the desk, and closed my eyes as if I could summon the sound of my father's voice.

I could not, and pulled the note from the next envelope.

Dearest Anne,

I have told you all, and hold you in confidence. It is a sad situation for which I see no hope, no other choice …

Each letter began in that manner, as their affair began and then continued over the months that followed. He wrote of their stolen moments together, a trip to the country during the summer that included an excuse to her husband that she was visiting family.

Then, a change in the tone of a letter dated that October.

Dearest Anne,

You must believe that I want to be with you, but cannot. There are so many other considerations …

I looked up from the letter. Considerations? Our mother? Linnie and myself? There had been no mention of us in the other letters.

Had she let him know there was a child all those months later when she returned from France, according to those documents and that registration of birth?

By then, our mother was gone.

Was it grief that had sent my father to the stables that day? The possibility of a scandal, along with the debts?

I refolded the letters and returned them to the envelopes, then looked up at a sound on the landing as Brodie returned.

That dark gaze met mine as he entered the office.

"I've informed Sir Avery that I am stepping away from the Talmadge inquiry."

"I would think that he was not pleased," I replied with more than a little surprise as I brushed the rain from the shoulders of his coat. A different expression then, not quite a smile nor a frown.

"He was not."

That dark gaze met mine, then his arms went around me.

"Are ye all right?" he asked as he had the night before.

I laid my head against his shoulder, his heart beating strong beneath my hand on the front of his coat.

I nodded.

He looked at that certificate of birth from over twenty years earlier. "It is worn and smeared, though the date is there: a girl, born 10 April of the following year, in France."

After he returned to the office, he spent the next hours reading the letters as well as the documents my great aunt had received.

"At the registrar's office in Compiègne," I replied, indicating the faint stamp at the bottom that was equally faded.

"Does this name mean anything to you?" He pointed out the faint signature in a tiny, precise scrawl above that barely legible stamp.

"It could be the signature of the local magistrate or possibly someone who attended the birth. I have heard there are places where women might go privately to have a child. Particularly in a situation that might not be acceptable in proper society."

"Aye, *proper society*," he repeated with no attempt to hide the disgust he felt.

I knew his thoughts ... that glaring difference between the classes where a woman of means might go to have a child in private and safety, while a woman of the poorer classes would be forced to have her child in some cold, rat-infested tenement.

"Where do ye want to begin?"

"I would like to know more about this woman, even though she's only been back in London for a short time. And about Lady Grantham." I knew there was always more to know about a person.

The Grantham name was not unknown. There had to be records for Sir Grantham: record of marriage, any other births, deaths, that sort of thing.

In addition, he had been a successful merchant as well as a member of Parliament. There were undoubtedly other members who knew him, and knew the family. There might be something there that could help us learn the truth.

"I will begin tomorrow with the Office of Official Records. There might also be something in the newspaper archives."

"And I will see wot might be learned through those associated with the Agency. They have sources that might be able to provide something," Brodie added.

"I don't imagine that Sir Stanton would approve of that, since you have stepped away from the Talmadge inquiry."

"No," Brodie admitted. "But young Mr. Sinclair might be able to assist."

Alex Sinclair was a young associate with the Agency, quite brilliant with his inventions and with a fascination for the more dangerous aspects of the Agency's work. He had proven himself to be quite valuable, surprisingly talented with a weapon that had surprised him as well, and he could keep a secret regarding some of those experiences.

There was much to do and I was most eager to begin.

"Wot of the showing of yer sister's paintings this evenin'?"

"I suppose there is very little that might be accomplished this afternoon," I replied, given the late hour with most offices I wanted to visit closing within a very short while.

"And I know the gallery showing is most important to her. We should attend as planned. She would be terribly disappointed if we did not."

I caught the expression on his face. More a grimace, I thought.

"It will be good for you," I added. "It will broaden your intellectual horizons."

The grimace was still there.

"Ye are the only one who could persuade me to attend such a thing. I would much rather spend the evening *alone* with ye.
"

I laid my hand against the front of his shirt, just there where it lay open.

"Afterward, Mr. Brodie," I promised him.

His hand closed around mine and he pressed a kiss against my fingers.

"I will hold ye to the bargain."

Attending a gallery showing did require more appropriate attire in consideration of the prestige of the gallery and those who would be attending.

We returned to Mayfair where I had moved most of his clothes under much protest.

It made no sense to keep two wardrobes of clothes, limited as his were—by choice—and had simply taken the matter into my own hands and had everything packed up except for his 'street clothes,' as he called them.

The situation was finally discovered as we prepared to decamp to Old Lodge and he had inquired about his long boots, which would undoubtedly be necessary in the cooler, often mucky climes in the north.

I had informed him that they were at the townhouse, along with his long overcoat, woolen trousers, and shirts.

I've heard about this sort of thing, he had declared at the time. *I suppose next ye'll be purchasing silk underdrawers and a nightshirt for me to wear.*

Silly man.

Not at all, I had assured him at the time. *A nightshirt would not do at all.*

Ye are a wanton woman, he had replied. And that had ended the conversation.

My housekeeper Mrs. Ryan had provided an early supper. I now stood in the doorway of the dressing room adjacent to the bedroom.

I had laid out the appropriate attire for him for the evening —the wool dress suit that he had previously worn once, white linen shirt, brocade vest, and tie.

He was presently standing in the middle of the room, quite

impressive, in trousers, shirt, and vest, and a glare as he struggled with the tie.

That glare fastened on me as I brushed his hands aside and proceeded to tie his tie, then fanned the flared ends out.

"Another of yer many talents," he commented. "Which might raise the question where ye learned such a thing."

"Aunt Antonia is a source of amazing information," I replied.

"And no doubt a woman of some experience."

I nodded. "There are rumors."

That dark gaze narrowed in a way I was most familiar with, and I took a step back.

"The driver will be here quite soon."

The gallery was in Westminster very near Mayfair, at the Mews, an elaborate concrete and stone building with marble columns that framed the entrance, and contained iron girders to protect it against fires that had ravaged London more than once in the past.

It had been privately funded and built over twenty years earlier, and my great aunt had been one of the founding donors. She had insisted that had nothing to do with the invitation for my sister to display her paintings. That had come independently from the board that oversaw the gallery.

The Grosvenor Gallery was actually several galleries housed in the building with that main entrance on New Bond Street, that included the East and West galleries of more traditional well-known artists, the Sculpture Gallery, and the Water Color Gallery, where the reception for Linnie's paintings was being held this evening.

We arrived in good time, a considerable number of other

guests entering the gallery. I was enormously pleased for my sister.

With encouragement from her husband, James, she had returned to her painting the past year with what could only be described as artistic passion. She had completed several new pieces that were to be included, along with others that had been stored away at Sussex Square during a difficult period.

We entered the gallery and gradually made our way past the library, then downstairs to the galleries.

The Water Color gallery was not as large as the main galleries, due to what Linnie had described as the smaller but growing interest in the medium—watercolors as opposed to oil paintings. But the location was equally impressive with a domed ceiling.

There were other artists' works displayed on the walls, but my sister's collection had been given particular placement at the entrance and then again on a raised carpet dais with one or two paintings along the way. It was a very special occasion for her.

Linnie, with James at her side, was nearby in conversation with an older gentleman—Sir Ponsonby, one of the owners of the gallery. He gazed about, and seemed most pleased with the number of people who filled the gallery.

"It seems that her ladyship has already arrived as well." Brodie pointed out my great aunt, surrounded by at least a dozen acquaintances, including Sir Laughton and his wife, much like a queen holding court

I was not surprised. Her family line went back several hundred years to King William, along with several other assorted royals along the way. And there was almost nothing she liked better than praising the accomplishments of our family.

I did wonder how she explained my ventures in assisting Brodie with his inquiry cases.

I then discovered Lily, standing before a display of four framed watercolors that represented the seasons of the year in the same garden in France that I recognized from my sister's earlier efforts. They were each quite beautiful, with a faint misty quality in the one that was meant to portray rain, while the painting that was labeled Spring Returns glowed with the promise of new flowers should a young woman stroll through a garden.

"Linnie started the first the first one when we were at school in Paris. I couldn't draw a simple figure to save myself, while this painting was presented before the class by our art instructor," I explained as I joined Lily.

"That must have been horrible. What did you do?"

"I managed to convince the headmistress that I was quite ill, then left the school."

"Where did you go?"

That was a conversation for another time. As Brodie often pointed out, she was very like me in spite of the fact that there was no blood relation, and could be quite bold.

"What do you think of the paintings?" I suggested instead, a diversion to be certain.

"Four seasons?" she replied. "There are only two at Old Lodge, and three here in London when the rains let up."

I laughed. I was much in agreement. In London the three seasons were rain, a warm month or two, then more rain. In Scotland the seasons had the reputation of being cold and colder, with a great deal of rain or snow, and a few hours of spring in the mix just to tease everyone.

Of course that was a bit of an exaggeration.

We continued our exploration of the gallery. As we encountered people I was acquainted with, I made introductions. I was quite impressed with Lily's polite responses. Particularly with Lady Dalrymple, who stared back at her through her lorgnette much like I had seen Mr. Brimley staring through his magnifying glass at a specimen. Her son, Horton, who had to be at least sixty years old and had never married, dithered beside her.

I did detect that faint roll of Lily's eyes, as we quickly moved on to the next part of the exhibit. I was much in agreement.

"What about this painting?" she asked as we gradually made our way around to where my great aunt stood with James, a woman I recognized as Mrs. Elnora Keating, and a handful of others.

Brodie stood nearby in conversation with a gentleman he was obviously acquainted with. As the man turned to acknowledge something Brodie said, I realized that it was Sir Avery Stanton from the Agency.

"Those are the gardens at Aunt Antonia's chateau at Chédigny in France," I explained.

She looked at me with a frown. "Chateau?"

"It's more of a country house with vineyards," I explained.

"The wine that Munro has brought from France," she observed as she continued to study the painting. *"C'est magnifique,"* she commented.

Her expertise of the French language was definitely improving in spite of declaring that she had no use for another language. I smiled.

It was most interesting to overhear some of the comments made about Linnie's paintings as we continued around the gallery, all of them quite complimentary.

I was pleased for her, considering she had been forced to

step away from her painting during her former marriage. Now James was so supportive of her, and as I glanced over at her in conversation with a gentleman and a woman—presumably his wife, although one could never tell—I could see what all of this meant to her. It was quite a triumph.

We continued about the gallery and gradually approached where I had first seen Aunt Antonia in conversation with those about her. As we approached closer, Lily took hold of my arm.

"What is it?"

"That's her!" she said as she stared past me.

"Whatever are you talking about?"

"The woman I saw outside the bookstore!"

Lily had been most adamant about the encounter.

The woman's interest in books, artwork, and now she had the boldness to approach Aunt Antonia directly.

She was dressed in a dark green satin gown with a dark green overcoat, and her hair was swept up into a thick cascade of waves of dark hair ... *dark auburn* hair.

Sir Laughton made my great aunt aware that we approached, in a tone I had heard before, but only in his profession as legal counsel, as with the day before at Sussex Square.

"Lady Forsythe," he said then. "Please make the acquaintance of ..."

The woman who stood with them turned, held out her hand, and made her own introduction.

"Victoria Grantham."

Five

LILY'S HAND tightened on my arm.

"It is perhaps somewhat premature," the woman suggested, "yet I wanted to see the exhibit, and of course I hoped that Lady Montgomery would be here as well."

Perhaps premature, I thought when we had only just received word of her claim.

"And you are Mikaela Forsythe, of course—your travels, books, and your private inquiry work. It is well known and fascinating."

"Lady Mikaela Forsythe," Lily announced and made no effort to disguise the tone in her voice.

"And this would be?"

"Miss Lily Montgomery Forsythe." Aunt Antonia made the formal introduction.

There was faint surprise and a smile, and I was immediately fascinated by the resemblance Lily had described. It was there in the woman's features—a similarity in the curve of her face, her nose, the manner in which she looked back at me now, and the color of her hair very near my own.

Was it possible that she was the daughter of my father's affair with another woman?

"Mikaela! The most exciting news ...!"

I heard the almost breathless excitement in Linnie's voice, then the small sound that followed as she joined us.

"Oh ..."

For myself, there was surprise, shock, and disbelief that the woman had made an appearance here, on an occasion that should have been about Linnie's success.

Aunt Antonia, with vast experience and expertise in navigating social challenges, was the lady of the hour as she rescued the situation.

"What is your news?"

Linnie stared at the woman, then recovered somewhat.

"I've been asked to exhibit in May by Monsieur de Laudier from the gallery in Paris. I didn't know that he would be here this evening."

The Paris Gallery. I remembered it from our school days and endless visits that I endured. Linnie had dreamed of one day having an exhibit there. It was quite prestigious, with many artists' works then included in the Louvre.

"I seem to have interrupted the conversation ..." Linnie started to apologize.

"Not at all," I assured her and reached out a hand to squeeze hers. "It is wonderful news, and the reason we are here tonight."

I was not usually the one to smooth over awkward situations. Aunt Antonia often said that the elite French finishing school I had attended had very likely been wasted on me. I was usually more direct and outspoken.

However, this was not about me, nor was it about the woman who stood across from me.

This was Linnie's time, one that she had worked hard for, then had her earlier efforts dashed by someone who thought more of himself than her. That was in the past, this was now. She should be able to enjoy the moment, and there was her condition to consider as James took her arm in silent support.

Brodie had quietly joined us, standing just behind my great aunt, his expression void of any emotion—his *inspector face*, I called it.

It was not his way to interfere in 'family matters,' as he called them. His own manner of dealing with things could be quite direct, in the way of the police inspector he had once been.

Except for that gaze that now met mine, in support I had learned to read and understand.

"Miss Grantham." Sir Laughton entered the somewhat uncomfortable situation. "There will be time enough later for conversations. This is neither the appropriate time, nor the place."

She stiffened.

"I do apologize," she replied. "I should have perhaps waited ..."

"Yes," Aunt Antonia replied in a voice that could turn water to ice.

Victoria Grantham nodded. "You will forgive me. It is only that to now have family that I never knew. It is most remarkable ..." She turned to me.

"And your successes as well as your inquiry business—most fascinating, I am envious. I can only hope that we may talk about all of this very soon."

I nodded. She turned and bid everyone good evening.

"Good heavens!" Linnie exclaimed. "Did you know that

she would be here?" She directed the question to our great aunt.

"Not at all," Aunt Antonia replied, then turned to Sir Laughton.

"You might be able to assist in this situation."

"Of course. I will see the matter taken care of. However, you do realize that there will need to be a meeting, considering the claim that she has made."

"All in due time," Aunt Antonia replied.

No translation was needed. This particular encounter was over.

And Lily, never at a loss, "That one is too bold," she commented, staring in the direction Victoria Grantham had made her departure. "I've seen ones like her before. They're always out to better themselves."

Outspoken most certainly. As a diversion, I suggested that Linnie explain her technique for creating her particular style of painting. That was met with a slight roll of the eyes—Lily's.

The exhibition closed at ten o'clock in the evening; however it would continue for a month. And then there was that invitation for my sister to exhibit her paintings in Paris.

In spite of the evening's encounter, Linnie 'soldiered on,' as the old saying goes, though she did pull me aside as the guests departed and we prepared to leave.

"What if her claim is genuine?" she asked.

"We shall cross that bridge when we come to it," I replied. "You are not to worry. You have yourself to think of and that forthcoming exhibit."

She gave me a knowing look.

"You're going to make inquiries about her," she concluded.

"Of course," Aunt Antonia commented as she and Lily prepared to leave for Sussex Square.

She smiled and nodded to Brodie where he stood beside me.

"I would expect nothing less."

"Her ladyship can be very masterful with only a few words," Brodie drily commented as he attempted to loosen his tie after our return to the townhouse.

There was, of course, a curse or two in the process. I crossed the dressing room and pushed his hands aside before the knot could be hopelessly tightened and require scissors to remove.

"You thought she would simply accept this woman's claim?" I replied as I worked the silk fabric loose. I looked up and found him watching me. "You should know better. She will want answers."

"Aye. I have had some experience with that."

I finally freed the knot from his tie.

He wrapped a hand around mine, then brushed stray hair back from my cheek with the other.

"Where will you begin?" he asked.

"My father undoubtedly had a circle of friends at his club, perhaps gambling partners. I will make inquiries there. After all, he lost a great deal of money there in the past."

"The past can be ... difficult."

I must admit I was not looking forward to it. This was very much like opening a door that was closed a long time ago.

"Gentlemen's Clubs are not the sort of place where a lady should go."

"Aunt Antonia will undoubtedly remember who some of his acquaintances were at the time. I'll start there."

"Aye. And there is someone who might be able to tell us something about those documents."

Someone? Undoubtedly someone from his 'other' life. I had discovered there were a considerable number of them.

"Does this person have a name?"

"He goes by the name The Forger. Mr. Cavendish might be able to assist in finding him. He keeps on the down-low due to the nature of his business."

The Forger. Most interesting. It was one of his acquaintances I had not met before.

"He's been known to assist those needing letters of transit and other documents."

"And you just happen to know him."

There was that smile.

"It is possible that I might have needed his services in the past."

I learned something new about Brodie from time to time. It did keep life most interesting.

I telephoned my great aunt after Brodie left for the office on the Strand to learn what Mr. Cavendish might know about where The Forger could be found. He did have his ear to the street, as they say, and usually knew where someone might be located in the East End.

"Clubs?" Aunt Antonia echoed my question. "That would be Brooks, dear."

It was well known in the family that she had breached that 'sacred male bastion.'

"The membership now is members of Parliament, and others of some means. Quite boring."

"There was Boodles and White's, of course. It was Constance Abberfeldy's scheme when we were a bit younger—a club a night, to see what was inside those sinful places. You remember Constance? She has passed on, but oh the adventures we shared. Her husband didn't approve of our "ladies' nights out and about." And no wonder. Ha! So, she rid herself of him. As for your father ...

"It was no secret that he spent a great amount of time at Brooks. On more than one occasion he was delivered home to the residence he shared with your mother at the time, by a driver from Brooks." She paused on the other end of the telephone call.

"Henry Portman was a name your mother mentioned. That would be 2nd Viscount Portman, and then Sir George Trevelyan. They were both members of Brooks at the same time. Your mother mentioned there was some financial arrangement between your father and Trevelyan, a loan perhaps.

"I am acquainted with Trevelyan's wife, Lady Genevieve, and Sir Laughton may be able to assist with Portman. At last, I am able to assist in one of your inquiry cases. This is so very exciting."

That did give me pause. I had always attempted to keep family out of our inquiry cases, unless absolutely necessary. Granted, I had not always been successful in that, particularly when it came to Lily. And admittedly I had relied on information from my great aunt on more than one occasion.

It was not the first time she had spoken of it. And of course, there was the matter of Lily, who seemed quite determined to learn more about becoming an inquiry agent.

For now, I had the names of two men who were acquainted

with my father at the time he supposedly had an affair with Anne Grantham.

What might they be able to tell me? Still, a better question might be, what would they be *willing* to tell me?

Men's clubs about London had the reputation of being most secretive about their membership and activities. I knew this from a previous case.

As for questions from a woman about such things?

I was prepared to use my great aunt's social position as well as my own, although, as Brodie had warned, I might learn things I would rather not know. And then there was the pain and anger that had never gone away. This was not going to be easy, for so many reasons.

After my conversation with my great aunt, I then decided to call on my brother-in-law. Linnie had been greatly upset by the previous evening's encounter and knew that I was going to be making inquiries. Before parting the night before, she insisted that I inform her what I might learn.

I had reluctantly agreed.

I had Mrs. Ryan call for a cab, then dressed for my meeting with James Warren.

I arrived at his office just as he had finished a meeting with his staff.

"Do come in. So good to see you again. After last evening I wasn't certain whether this would be professional or personal."

"Personal," I replied. "I will be making inquiries regarding the woman's claim."

He sat behind his desk as I had seen him do dozens of times as my publisher, always relaxed, curious, and supportive. However, this was different.

"Yes, Linnie told me."

"My first concern is for her," I explained. "Even though she has insisted that she wants to know everything I'm able to learn."

"I understand, and I appreciate that," he replied. "This child is very special for her, for both of us."

"Therefore," I continued, "I would hope that you might assist in this."

There was a moment of surprise. "Of course, in whatever way I can."

"As Brodie and I are able to learn something that might be important, I would very much prefer to share it with you first, whatever that might be. It might perhaps be more easily heard from you. Not in great detail, of course, yet ..."

"A carefully edited version?" he suggested, with one elbow braced on the arm of his chair, chin resting on one hand.

That was precisely the word for it.

"We have only been married a few months," he replied. "However, I have learned a great deal about your sister in that time. She is very perceptive and can be somewhat stubborn about things. I believe the two of you share that." He was thoughtful.

"I will agree to this, but you must be aware that she will have questions, and I will not keep anything from her. I will not have her hurt or distressed over the matter, and risk her health or that of our child. If there is something that would be better for her to know afterward, then I would ask that you keep it for yourself and Mr. Brodie."

"I am counting on her being preoccupied with the forthcoming exhibit in Paris, as well," I pointed out.

He nodded. "I'm not certain just how that will work. The baby is due the first part of April."

I smiled. "You did mention that she is stubborn. I am confident that she will manage both quite well."

There are things I suppose everyone would rather leave in the past, most certainly myself.

Yet, here I was setting off on my own inquiries, about to open the door on my childhood and all the pain and other emotions that went with it.

That day, very near twenty years earlier, I had yelled and cursed at my father. Although admittedly, my vocabulary in that regard was somewhat limited at the time.

I remember the anger, the feeling of helplessness, questions that could never be answered. There certainly had been no answer from my father's lifeless body after he took his life. And so, I had locked everything from that day away.

Now I was opening that door on the past in an attempt to find out who Victoria Grantham was.

Brodie understood, more than I suppose anyone could. He had his own painful memories.

I returned to the townhouse after meeting with James Warren.

Mrs. Ryan met me at the door.

"You have two messages brought round earlier. They're on your desk."

I recognized one of the envelopes. It was from Sir Laughton. However, I did not recognize the second one. I opened the one from Sir Laughton.

He had made contact with Viscount Portman, and let him know that it was an important matter with a request to meet with me. The meeting was arranged for that afternoon at the office the Viscount maintained at Parliament.

Sir Laughton would continue to attempt to reach the other two men my great aunt had mentioned who had acquaintance with my father all those years before, as well as membership at Brooks Club.

The meeting with Viscount Portman was for four o'clock, after members would be adjourning for the day.

I was familiar with the sprawling buildings at the river that were part of Parliament, and had just enough time to eat the luncheon Mrs. Ryan set out and then change my clothes for my meeting with him.

I hastily opened the second envelope. It was from Victoria Grantham. Her greeting momentarily stopped me:

Dear Mikaela,

I realize our meeting at the gallery was somewhat difficult last evening. I apologize.

I want only to know my family after so many secrets and so much sadness. It is something that I know you must understand as well.

It is my hope that we might meet in private. Please send your response to my representative.

I look forward to seeing you.

Victoria Grantham Forsythe

I had to agree with Lily. That was too bold, already asserting herself by using the Forsythe name.

Was she in fact my sister? With the little I remembered of my father, the possibility of an affair was not impossible. And a child born from that affair?

I returned the note to the envelope and called to Mrs. Ryan that I would need a driver for an appointment. I then tucked both envelopes into my bag, and went upstairs to change for my meeting with Viscount Portman.

The houses of Parliament, the House of Commons and the House of Lords, were located in the Palace of Westminster. The oldest part of the palace was Westminster Hall, built during the reign of King William, an ancestor according to my great aunt.

Over the centuries as the demands of government expanded, alterations were made that included a library, new law courts, meeting halls, and the private residence for the Speaker of the House of Commons.

It was built of sand-colored limestone and dominated the left bank of the Thames, with a number of small gardens and the green that extended down to the riverbank.

It was a maze of meeting rooms that included the robing room, long halls, the Queen's Hall, and was said to contain over two hundred private offices for the members.

I had not been back to visit since a previous inquiry case with Brodie. As my driver angled the cab around to the main entrance, I noticed there were still faint powder marks—gun powder, that is, from that previous case—on one wall that led down to the river.

Word had been sent down to the clerk's office inside the main entrance regarding my appointment. I signed in and was then given directions to Viscount Portman's office.

There were lifts throughout to accommodate the number of people who worked here. They were connected by a maze of stairways. It had made navigating the building in that previous case most interesting.

If I had not been there previously, I might have become

lost. As it was, I arrived at the clerk's desk outside the office of the Viscount in time for our meeting. Once again, I signed in with the clerk, a measure put in place after threats were made in the past against certain members of Parliament.

The clerk announced my arrival, and I was immediately shown into the Viscount's office.

Viscount Portman was a stout man of medium height with graying brown hair, side-whiskers, and a pale blue gaze beneath the overhang of thick brows. I thanked him for meeting with me with no previous appointment and on such short notice.

He rose from behind his desk and circled round, then offered me a chair before the desk.

"I must say that I was most curious when I received Sir Laughton's request that I meet with you."

During the ride from Mayfair, I had been rehearsing what I might say when I met with the Viscount. I was fully aware that he might be reluctant or simply refuse to discuss things that were over twenty years old.

"There is a matter that affects my family, including my great aunt, Lady Antonia Montgomery." Never let it be said that I was opposed to using family influence when necessary. "It is my hope that you might be able to provide information that could be helpful regarding your friendship with my father, Sir John Forsythe."

That one word, *father*, caught slightly. I pushed past it.

I watched him as I explained the reason for my request to meet, and saw the slow breath he took as he studied me.

"Lady Forsythe," he repeated. "After the previous situation here at Westminster Hall that you assisted in thwarting, I considered that it must be most important even though it is somewhat ... *surprising* for a lady to undertake such things. I do hope we are not facing another situation such as that, although it does seem that the world has become more dangerous."

It was not the first time I had heard that sort of comment regarding expectations for women. I ignored it.

"Not at all," I assured him. "This is more of a personal nature that I hope you can assist with."

His expression was mildly perplexed. "In any way that I may. But first, you must tell me about Lady Montgomery. I hope that she is well."

"Very well, and it is with her insistence that I requested the meeting. She does hold you in high regard."

"Of course," he replied. "Although I do not know how I may assist in the dear lady's affairs."

"There is a somewhat delicate matter that has been brought to the attention of the family, and it is hoped that you might be able to provide some information, regarding Sir John Forsythe."

Once again, I caught that faint change of expression that was quickly masked.

"A sad situation, a very long time ago. My sympathy to you and Lady Montgomery."

I was not after sympathy.

"I am aware that you both belonged to the Brooks Club."

His expression changed to mild curiosity.

"Yes, as I remember it, we had joined about the same time. You seem to be well informed."

I didn't bother to explain that my great aunt had *attended* the club with Constance Abberfeldy, both dressed as men.

"Undoubtedly there are things that gentlemen would share over a game of cards, or brandy."

That curiosity sharpened to some other reaction.

"As ladies undoubtedly do when they get together and

gossip about things. What precisely is the *'matter'* you speak of?" he asked.

There was no polite way to say it, other than to say it.

"A young woman by the name of Victoria Grantham has come forward and made the claim that John Forsythe was her father."

"Grantham, the name is familiar," he repeated. "He was once a member of Parliament."

I nodded and continued on.

"Naturally, it is important for our family to determine the truth of the situation, as I am certain you can well understand. In view of your acquaintance with Sir John Forsythe as well as shared experiences at Brooks, it is possible that something may have been known of the *situation*. Something that should be spoken of ... between men."

He stiffened noticeably.

"And you are here to learn what might have been spoken of over a game of cards," he replied in a measured tone, as he drummed his fingers on the desktop.

Several moments passed. I made an attempt to ease the difficult conversation with an apology or some other comment, as he continued to drum away.

"I understand the need to protect one's reputation ..." he began. "Yet, I would remind you that it has been more than twenty years since your father's tragic death."

He stood then. "You have my sympathies, Lady Forsythe and Lady Montgomery as well; however, I cannot assist in this. Surely you understand, after all this time ... You must give my regards to Lady Montgomery."

Sympathies? Cannot assist? An answer, and yet no answer at all.

It was obvious that I had come up against that typical attitude of men, of protecting their own.

He was clearly choosing not to discuss what he knew, and our meeting was at an end.

"Insufferable! Arrogant! Bloody ass!"

Brodie looked at me with some surprise as I paced back and forth across the office.

"What did ye expect?" he asked. "That he would tell ye if yer father spoke openly of an affair?"

"I *hoped* that, in consideration of the situation, he might have been willing to share something that might have passed in conversation between them, particularly in view of Aunt Antonia's considerable influence."

"Did ye now?"

I looked over at where he sat behind the desk, insufferably handsome in a black jumper with turtleneck over rough work pants, that made him look very much like someone who might make off with the Crown Jewels. Most stirring. And I was not in the mood to be stirred! At least not in that way.

I had already told him of my visit with the Viscount, along with the letter from Victoria Grantham.

"Insufferable louts!" I repeated. "Men discussing their conquests over drink and card games," I added. "And who knows what else in private rooms. But it must be kept secret."

Brodie continued to watch me with that aggravating, slightly amused expression.

"The least he could have done was to confirm or deny there had been an affair," I pointed, quite logically. "Men do discuss those things. Their conquests?"

"And the ladies do not?" Brodie replied.

When I would have denied any such thing, I had to stop myself. I had never indulged in that sort of thing, but I thought of Aunt Antonia. Very definitely a woman ahead of her time in that regard, sneaking into men's clubs and that sort of thing.

I threw myself into the chair opposite the desk and glared at him.

"Are ye quite through now?" he asked in that maddening way he had when I was stirred up about something.

"I'm getting there."

"It's possible that I had a bit more success with The Forger."

"You were able to find him?'

"Mr. Cavendish was able to find where he's now set up shop, so to speak. Ye have him to thank for it."

He spread one of the documents across the desk. I knew what he was doing, of course. He was distracting me.

"What was he able to tell you?"

"The record of residence at the *'private home'* in France would seem to be a copy. The ink is not as old as on the registration of birth.

"That might be authentic, although it's written in French. That was more difficult to determine, as the official stamp on the paper appears to have suffered some damage. He was able to determine that something had been spilled across it and distorted the stamp so that it was impossible to read the information.

"But there's more," he continued. "A name that appears to have been added to the birth registration sometime after—the name of the father."

There was no need to explain further. I knew the name on the document.

"Was he certain?" I asked.

"Aye, for a few more shillings."

"Do you trust him?"

"He would have no reason to lie and every reason to hope for continued business in the future."

The question now was, who had added John Forsythe's name? Victoria Grantham, after she found the letters? In an attempt to prove her claim? Yet the larger question remained, why after all this time?

She had been living in France, according to what she told us, and had returned when her mother was taken ill and then died, with Sir Grantham's death several years before.

"Wot will you do about the woman's request?" Brodie asked.

I wasn't yet ready to meet with her. I needed to know more.

There was another person I wanted to meet with—Lady Genevieve Trevelyan. According to Aunt Antonia, Sir George Trevelyan had been a close friend of my father and had apparently made a loan to him for some amount.

To cover mounting gambling debts? Or for some other reason? Perhaps Anne Grantham's extended stay in France?

Was it possible that Lady Trevelyan knew something about it?

What would she be willing to tell me?

VERY LITTLE IT SEEMED, as I was informed by a very brief note in response, that Lady Trevelyan's schedule was quite full and she could not possibly meet with me.

"I see," Aunt Antonia replied, when I spoke of it. "It does seem as if it might be necessary for me to send round a note to persuade her. And," she had added for emphasis, "as I recall the Viscount is hoping for an appointment to the House of Lords, with the recent death of Lord Bruce Carmichael ... such a pity, such a dear man."

"Aye, politics," Brodie commented when he heard of my great aunt's response. "I've experienced her ladyship first-hand when she is determined to make something happen."

Within an hour of sending round her personal footman with a note, I received a telephone call at the townhouse from Lady Trevelyan's personal secretary, informing me that her ladyship would be pleased to meet with me at Slater's in Piccadilly, where she was to meet with her ladies in the Tea Room.

It appeared that Brodie was correct. No one could have

lived as long as my great aunt with such great influence, and not learned how to use that influence.

I arrived at Slater's at the appointed time and went downstairs to the Tea Room, where a waiter directed me to Lady Trevelyan's table. Her ladies had obviously not yet arrived. She sat alone.

She was an elegant woman, of the age my mother might have been had she lived. Her dark hair was swept up and fastened atop her head, her eyes gray as she greeted me with a polite smile.

"It was most pleasant speaking with Lady Montgomery," she commented. "A formidable woman. I do hope that she is well."

"Quite well," I replied, "and formidable indeed."

We exchanged a few brief pleasantries about people we both knew, and the gloomy winter weather that had set in. She paused as the waiter served tea. I waited as she added lemon, stirred, then set her spoon back on the saucer.

"Her ladyship spoke of a family matter of some importance and thought I might be of assistance, although I cannot imagine how that might be. However, I will help in any way that I can."

Once again, I had rehearsed just how I might approach the delicate subject of an affair between my father and Lady Grantham with those who might have been within the circle of acquaintances.

"It is a rather delicate matter. A situation that occurred several years ago and is now a matter of importance to our family."

I explained by first mentioning that three men, including my father and the Viscount, had been members of Brooks Club.

"Brooks," she sniffed with obvious disdain. "That was indeed a very long time ago. My husband prefers White's now, as several members of Parliament are also members there." She lifted her cup and took a long sip of tea.

"This would be regarding something Sir John Forsythe might have shared with the Viscount in confidence," I continued. "Regarding his ... *acquaintance* with a woman by the name of Lady Anne Grantham."

I caught the look on Lady Trevelyan's face as she very carefully set her cup back on the saucer.

"You flatter me in thinking that I would know of such things ... rumors, gossip ... there is always something of that sort going about, and best to disregard it.

"Affairs are not unusual," she continued. "But the consequences can be devastating."

The way she said it, I did wonder if she might have experienced a similar situation.

"Lady Grantham's daughter has now come forward with the claim that Sir John Forsythe, not Sir Grantham, was her father." I caught the change in her expression, the manner in which she folded her hands in her lap.

"I am certain that you can appreciate that it is most important to my great aunt to determine the validity of her claim," I added.

"Of course," she replied, then suddenly looked past me. "My ladies have arrived," she announced, then stood and laid down her napkin. "What you've shared is an unfortunate situation, but there is nothing I can tell you."

Considering her manner, her carefully chosen words, and now an abrupt end to our conversation, I was convinced that she knew something about all of this, but it was obvious she was not going to share whatever that might be.

As her *ladies* arrived at the table, I thanked her for meeting with me and left, aware of the curious stares that followed me.

'Let them eat cake,' I thought.

I found a cab and asked the driver to take me to the *Times* newspaper building. In the past I had been able to find valuable information in our inquiry cases. The *Times* of London, among other publications, had begun to archive past issues of their newspapers on film rather than storing decades of copies that gradually deteriorated over time.

It was a fascinating process, and had made my task far easier when looking for information about an event or someone whose activities appeared on the gossip sheets.

What might I find on those gossip sheets about Lady Grantham's extended stay in France twenty years earlier?

I signed in at the ground floor desk, then took the lift to the second floor where the archive was located.

"Lady Forsythe," the man in the archive acknowledged. "A new inquiry case, no doubt. How may I help you today?" I did sense the faint undertone of disdain that I had encountered on previous occasions.

Instead of responding, I requested the film archive for the newspaper, beginning the year before my father's death in the hope that I might find something that would provide a clue to the question about the woman's claim.

Of course, I was aware that I might not care for what I would find.

It was tedious work that would have been far easier if there was a catalog system as in the British Library, where one could simply look up a person's name or some other reference and find related books and documents.

Without a catalog of articles in newspapers, there was

nothing to do but scan each issue of the paper, most particularly the gossip sheet.

4 June 1871

I read with some amusement an account about my great aunt. It was rumored that she had been seen at Boodles men's club, although the person who claimed to have seen her couldn't be certain as *the person was dressed as a man …*

Scandal, scandal. What had become of London Society? The author of that particular bit of gossip had asked. I could only smile at that.

"Well done." I commented to myself. Then …

11 June 1872.

The date of my father's death.

The comment on the gossip sheet referred to the death notice of Sir John Forsythe of London, in what appeared to be a '*hunting*' accident. And the next line that was written …

Sir Forsythe's body was found by his nine-year-old daughter. Most tragic! And further tragedy, it is rumored that the estate will be sold to pay Sir Forsythe's gambling debts, with two children now orphaned. There are rumors about what might have caused him to take his own life …

I forced myself past that and continued to scroll through two additional rolls of film, each one containing several weeks of copies of the newspaper. Therein I discovered when Sir

George Trevelyan had been elected to the House of Commons, Sir Henry Portman appointed to the House of Lords two years later.

I continued my search as the hours of the afternoon passed. And then …

In the society news, of 18 June 1892, I found a brief announcement that Miss Victoria Grantham, daughter of Lady Anne Grantham, had returned from France after an extended tour.

Five months earlier! And far different from the two months that Victoria Grantham had claimed, when she returned upon her mother's illness.

I sat back in the chair and stared at the gossip sheet on the viewer in front of me.

What reason would Victoria Grantham have to lie about when she had returned?

I wrote down the information in my notebook, then continued to scroll through the most recent film archive along with copies of recent issues that had not yet been photographed.

I found the announcement of the death of Lady Anne Grantham with burial that followed at Highgate Cemetery. Guests were noted to include Lady Victoria Grantham, servants, and a man whose name was not shown.

Victoria Grantham's representative, Jerrold Handley, perhaps? Or some other unnamed family member?

And an unexpected surprise.

The person who had been assigned to report on the funeral for the Times was none other than Theodolphus Burke.

There were several words that came to mind that might describe the man—ambitious, scheming, despicable, determined to get his story no matter the cost to others.

The man had proven himself absolutely ruthless to the extent that he had jeopardized a previous investigation and put a young woman's life at risk.

I had heard from Lucy Penworth, who had once worked at the Times before joining the Agency, that he had been demoted from his position as preeminent reporter for the newspaper after that inquiry case. It did appear that he was now assigned to writing about dead people.

Oh, how the mighty had fallen.

I couldn't image a better assignment for him. Yet, it did raise the possibility that he might have information about Lady Anne Grantham's funeral and the unnamed man who had attended.

As much as I loathed the man and had once hoped for his demise—I wouldn't have been opposed to inserting the blade myself and watching him bleed out, as they say—as much as I despised Burke, I would call on him in an attempt to learn what he might know.

The clerk announced that it was closing hour for the archive. I closed my notebook, then returned the last roll of film to the clerk at the desk. I left the Times building and waved down a cab.

I had learned several things, although it was impossible to know yet what any of it meant.

Lady Trevelyan had obviously refused to tell anything she might know. What did that mean? Was she protecting someone? If so, who? And for what reason?

The newspaper archive had revealed the difference in the date Victoria Grantham had returned to London, supposedly to care for her ailing mother. It had also revealed the mourners at Lady Anne Grantham's funeral had included a man—name not shown.

There was a light in the window of the office as I returned. Brodie had obviously returned from that earlier meeting.

Mr. Cavendish, née The Mudger, rolled out from the over-hang above the sidewalk on his platform, a unique method of transportation after losing both legs above the knees.

He was already dressed for the colder weather with a jacket —quite nattily in style, with a wool scarf about his neck and woolen cap.

Rupert the hound emerged as well, obviously awakened from a nap, stretched then approached, tail wagging.

I scratched him behind the ears. He was a fine fellow, once one looked past the smears and smudges, not to mention the smell, from his daily foray onto the streets of the East End in search of whatever might be found in refuse bins, or a hand-out from acquaintances along the Strand that included Miss Effie at the Public House.

"We were about to go for something to warm the bones," Mr. Cavendish commented.

Warming the bones usually included a couple of pints of beer for him and a plate of left-overs for Rupert.

"Mr. Brodie said to keep an eye out for you. Seems he has a bit of information on that new case."

Mr. Cavendish was always well-informed about our inquiry cases, even though Brodie rarely shared anything with him of that nature unless it was to assist with a particular case.

He most certainly had his own means of acquiring infor-mation from his sources on the streets.

He rang the service bell to announce my arrival. Then man and hound set off across the Strand, Mr. Cavendish wheeling himself through early evening traffic with terrifying speed, the hound bounding alongside.

"Here ye are," Brodie said as he came down the stairs from

the office. "We have an appointment that might be useful." He waved down a driver, then assisted me inside.

"An appointment? With whom?"

The ride was brief, and then the driver pulled to the curb outside the apothecary shop. Brodie shielded me with his umbrella as we entered the shop.

There was always the strong smell of formaldehyde, much like pickles, with the sharp odor of medicinal alcohol. Such were two of the tools of the trade of the chemist, Mr. Brimley.

He had once studied to be a physician. But circumstances had changed his direction, and he had chosen to work in the East End with his shop. Here he provided care for the people, most of whom could not always pay for his services, that included women who found themselves in a 'difficulty.'

He had assisted in past inquiry cases with his expertise, particularly with dead bodies and causes of death that had revealed clues.

I could also personally attest to his skill as a surgeon, after being shot in the course of that first inquiry case with Brodie.

He was also a good friend and greeted us now as he saw his assistant, Sara, to the door at the end of the work day.

"Your pay is in the envelope," he told her as he handed it to her. "And give that medicine to your friend. It will help ease the misery in his lungs."

He turned, peering at us over the top of his glasses.

"She calls him '*brother*,' but I suspect that he is more than that to her. Poor chap has lung disease. Nothing to be done but make him more comfortable. She knows it as well." That myopic gaze fastened on me.

"It is good to see you again, Miss Forsythe."

Then in that distracted way of his, he turned and led the way to the back of his shop that contained the press for making pills, along with powders, and tonic that lined the shelves, as well as a variety of specimens that he collected in jars that had included a severed hand, an eyeball, and usually some internal organ.

I did not ask how he acquired them.

He adjusted his glasses as we entered the back room. A handful of microscopes lined the counter at one side of the room, along with what appeared to be a specimen—removed from one of those jars, pinned to a board, and I presumed currently under investigation.

"I have it here, Mr. Brodie," he commented as he led us past the specimen, for which I was grateful.

Not that I was squeamish about such things. As a child, there was always some poor creature being brought back to our house in the country when our father went off to hunt with companions, on the rare occasions he was there.

And then there were the variety of specimens, usually missing a head, that Rupert brought back to the office on the Strand and proceeded to dismember in the alcove. The variety might include rats, castoff body parts from the butcher shop, or once an old boot with a foot still inside.

Mr. Cavendish had retrieved the foot and properly disposed of it, much to the hound's displeasure, with a comment at the time about losing one's foot. Or rather, both feet, as it were in his particular case.

Mr. Brimley now proceeded to a microscope at the far end of the counter and turned on the overhead light. One of the documents that had been provided by Victoria Grantham's representative in that initial envelope that Aunt Antonia received lay on the counter beside the microscope.

"I had a thought after you left," he explained with a look over at Brodie in that same faintly distracted manner.

He bent over the document, wisps of white hair spiking up around his head as he took off his glasses and donned a pair of goggles, much like the ones Aunt Antonia wore for protection from *flotsam and mud,'* when navigating about in her motor carriage.

Mr. Brimley grinned as he looked over at us, appearing very much like an enormous bug.

"I've improved the lenses," he explained. "So that I can see things far better than the microscope might reveal and in greater detail." He gestured to the document and went on to explain.

"I first looked at the paper under the microscope when you brought it over earlier today, Mr. Brodie. I then had a go at it with the goggles which revealed a great deal more."

"And the lemon juice ye mentioned?" Brodie inquired.

Mr. Brimley smiled as he explained.

"It is something I've experimented with before, and was very revealing. The lemon juice is highly acidic. When brushed over paper and heated at the same time it changes the composition of the paper and anything written on it. Of course, one does need to be careful not to set the paper afire." That smile again.

"I waited until you returned to demonstrate."

"By all means," I replied. I was most eager to see what might be revealed by those shadows we had seen on the document.

"Anything that emerges here will permanently mark the paper, and possibly overwrite anything else." He looked expectantly from me to Brodie.

"If there is something else on the document, I want to see it."

Mr. Brimley had set everything up for the *'experiment'* and proceeded to pour lemon juice from a bottle into a small bowl. He then added a small amount of water.

"For the heat, we might use your hand-held light, Mr. Brodie. Safer than a candle or one of my burners."

Brodie removed the lantern from his coat pocket as Mr. Brimley stirred the lemon and water mixture, then took a brush from a nearby jar.

"For this to work, you must hold the lamp under the document as the lemon water is applied."

Brodie held the lamp under the document as Mr. Brimley handed the brush to me.

"Very lightly now across the document where you hope to see more of that which is written, if you please, Lady Forsythe."

I took the brush from him and dipped it into the solution, then lightly brushed across the faded writing that had been entered on the document.

Remarkably, those shadows behind the faded letters on the document slowly began to emerge!

I looked over at Brodie.

What was hidden there? What might it tell us?

Along with that, for what reason had the document been written over? And by whom?

Seven

ONLY A FEW OF the letters hidden there gradually emerged, the acid of the lemon juice heated by the lamp slowly turning the paper a shade of brown and causing them to slowly disappear once more, one by one, into a dark stain on the paper.

I wrote down the few letters that I was able to decipher from the hodgepodge of curves and marks, very much like playing a word game, with most of the letters now faded into the dark brown cloud of the document.

"Are ye able to make anything of it?" Brodie asked as the experiment ended and he turned off the lamp.

"The letters make no sense and there are so few of them," I replied. It was disappointing to say the least.

I had no idea what I had hoped for or what any of it might mean.

Mr. Brimley obviously sensed my disappointment.

"Might it be in another language since the document is written in French?"

"Perhaps."

Brodie and I thanked him in spite of the fact that nothing conclusive had been revealed with Mr. Brimley's experiment, except for those few letters.

We returned to the office on the Strand. Brodie then went to the Public House to have Miss Effie prepare two supper boxes, although I had little appetite, while I remained and added what I had learned today on the blackboard.

Our inquiry cases usually included a crime—stolen documents, a threat against the Crown, spies, murder ...

Yet, here there was no crime. There was only Victoria Grantham's claim. That in itself, painful as it was to learn that my father may have had a child by another woman while my mother lay dying, was not a crime in itself.

The quick double ring of the telephone on Brodie's desk was startling in the quiet of the office.

Then it rang again as it took me a moment to reach the desk.

The call was from my housekeeper, Mrs. Ryan. She had received a note by courier from Sir Laughton. I asked her to open the envelope and read the note.

He had been contacted once again by Victoria Grantham's representative, with a request to meet with our family. Sir Laughton would be working late into the evening at his office and awaited our response.

There was no need to consult my great aunt. I knew very well what her response would be as she had already turned over the situation to me.

"To make your inquiries, dear."

As far as Linnie was concerned, I refused to bring her into this part of it, until I could determine the truth of the woman's claim.

I then placed a telephone call to Sir Laughton's office. He

answered promptly and inquired how he should respond to this new request.

"I will meet with Victoria Grantham," I replied. "And it is to be at the Grantham residence in Waverly Park."

He was not in favor of that, preferring a public place and suggesting his own office. I thanked him but insisted on the Grantham residence at Waverly for the location.

I had learned over the course of our cases that there was always something to be learned from a person's surroundings —the hidden part of Edinburgh beneath the city streets, a walk-up flat in the poor part of the East End, the flat of an actress brutally murdered, or the physician who kept secrets in the room behind his office.

I wanted to know what might be learned from the residence where Anne Grantham had lived before her death, and Victoria Grantham had before she left for France years before.

What might it tell me about the young woman who claimed to be the daughter of an affair my father had years before?

Something? Anything? Nothing?

Yet first, I wanted to meet with Theodolphus Burke and see what he might remember from Anne Grantham's funeral. As much as I loathed the man, he had built a reputation for detail that had always thrilled the readers of his weekly page in the *Times*—*Crimes about the City*. It was possible there was some detail that might be useful.

By the end of that brief conversation, Sir Laughton had agreed to convey my agreement to meet Victoria Grantham the following afternoon at Waverly Place. He would send round a message once it was confirmed.

"I dinna care for it," Brodie replied when he returned and I informed him about the proposed meeting.

He was very much against my meeting alone with Victoria Grantham, although he did acknowledge that it could be useful.

I also explained that I hoped to meet with Theodolphus Burke in the morning because of what I had read in that newspaper archive. I did not intend to schedule an appointment that the man could decline.

"Aye," Brodie eventually replied. "I shouldna have agreed to include ye in that first case over yer sister's disappearance."

"I do believe it is a little late for that," I told him. "And it was through my efforts, not to mention my family connections, that we were able to solve the case at all and prevent harm to the Royal family." He gave me that narrowed look.

"Perhaps."

"No *'perhaps'* to it." Bloody stubborn Scot. He had a very convenient memory when he chose.

"You must admit that I am right about this." End of discussion as far as I was concerned. Or possibly not, as far as the bloody stubborn Scot was concerned.

"Verra well, but ye'll not go alone. I will see you there and wait for ye until ye are finished with your meetin' with Miss Grantham."

Hmmm, yes. Quite stubborn.

It was very late when we finished the supper Miss Effie had provided from the Public House. He put more coal on the stove and then we retired for the night.

Still, it was some time before I slept. I kept turning over and over in my mind what we knew about Anne Grantham, her apparent affair with my father, and Victoria Grantham's claim.

It was like pulling the curtain back on ghosts of the past that I had worked very hard to leave in the past—our mother's death, then childhood feelings of having been abandoned, the horror of discovering our father dead, attempting to find some understanding of it all when there was no understanding to be had.

Not then. And now?

I got up and paced the outer office, then put more coal on the fire that had burned low. And Brodie was there, quite handsome with that dark mane of hair disheveled about his head, the shadow of that dark beard, those dark eyes that watched me through the shadows. Quite stirring, I thought, as I wiped the bloody tears from my cheek.

And I never cried! Almost never.

And he was still there, a bit blurry through the tears as his hand found mine. He pulled me down across his lap, and handed me a glass of my aunt's very fine whisky with just a wee dram.

"To help ye sleep, lass."

Bloody Scot, I thought as I sipped the whisky. He did know me quite well.

We dressed the following morning and returned to the town house in Mayfair. Sir Laughton's telephone call came just after the clock in the front parlor chimed the ten o'clock hour.

"It has been arranged for you to meet with Victoria Grantham at her residence, although I advise against it."

I did appreciate his concerns and informed him that Brodie would be accompanying me.

"There are many issues with this young woman's claim. You must let me know what you are able to learn afterward."

I had dressed for the day earlier while awaiting his call, and now asked Mrs. Ryan to call for a driver to take me to the

Times newspaper offices, where I hoped to meet with Theodolphus Burke.

Not for the first time, I did wonder who named their child that, and suspected once again that it was no doubt invented by Mr. Burke himself.

The arrogance of the man!

Brodie was confident that I could handle Mr. Burke and sent me off on my own with the agreement that he would meet me outside the Times offices by noon. That would leave more than enough time for my meeting with Victoria Grantham.

"I know how ye can be when ye have yer mind set," he commented in parting, with a brief kiss. "That should give ye enough time to *'persuade'* the man that his life is not worth holding back information for his own purposes."

He could be such a cheeky fellow.

The business offices, including the large writers' gallery where desks were crowded side-by-side on the second floor, were at a separate location from the building that held the archives.

I arrived in good time, considering the weather and the traffic, and at the time I hoped to find Burke still about when assignments were handed out to staff writers—including, I hoped, the latest noteworthy funeral that he would be given to write about.

I had been here before and passed by the first-floor clerk by informing him that I had an appointment, which of course I did not. But I refused to give Burke warning that I was there to see him as I climbed the stairs to the second floor. It would not be the first time he had simply left the building by way of another stairway to avoid meeting with me.

I reached the second floor and scanned the desks in the gallery. Even for someone who had never been there before or spoken with the man, he would have been easy to identify by the rolled-back shirt sleeves with garters, and overall appearance as if he might have slept in his clothes. The cigarette that hung out of his mouth was familiar sight as he gathered the package of more cigarettes, a box of wood matches by the label, and top hat—his signature calling card—and his long coat from the back of his chair.

"Good morning, Mr. Burke," I called out as I briskly crossed the gallery before he could get past me and disappear.

"A moment of your time, if you please. And it is so good to see you again."

My arrival brought up heads and caused stares from those others who had not yet departed the gallery with their daily assignment.

I was greeted by a series of curious glances, openly flirtatious stares, and a very audible groan as the only escape route was closed to him.

"To what do I owe this doubtful pleasure?" Burke snapped. "I was about to leave."

So charming, I thought. I had no idea how long it would take to ask my questions about the funeral of Lady Anne Grantham since that depended completely on him.

"I will only need a few minutes of your time."

Another groan.

"The private conference room?" I suggested. "Or here in the gallery?" Where his fellow writers would obviously eavesdrop on our conversation.

"The conference room if you please, Lady Forsythe," he replied with a nod of the head.

I had met here previously on another case, yet indicated for him to proceed ahead of me. I did not put it past him to escape at the last minute.

"I had heard that you were off on travels," he commented as we each went to a chair across the meeting table from each other.

Sarcasm. I was reminded that he was quite the expert at it.

"Perhaps in the spring." I played along. And then decided that flattery might work. If not, I was prepared to use other tactics.

Where Brodie and I often bandied comments, it was all in good humor. There was nothing humorous to a conversation with Mr. Burke. It was all about what was in it for him.

"As I was saying, to what do I owe the pleasure?" he repeated.

"It seems that you have come up in the ranks of journalism of late. I recently noted your reporting among the obituaries."

"A brief exercise, I assure you, gathering material for a book I may write about the profession of legitimate journalism, not the usual flotsam and gibberish that some write about."

Touché, I thought.

"What particular death notice caught your eye, if I may inquire. Working on something of your own, perhaps?"

I thought briefly of the revolver in my bag, then dismissed it. Brodie would not approve—there too many witnesses about.

"The funeral notice for Lady Anne Grantham was quite eloquent." Never let it be said that I was above flattery, even as the words very nearly caught in my throat.

"However," I continued, "It was missing a bit of information. That is so very unlike you. And since Lady Antonia is acquainted with the family ..." A slight exaggeration there. "She was concerned that someone may have been overlooked. As I say, so very unlike you."

His eyes narrowed.

"Such as, Lady Forsythe? As I recall, although it has been very near two months ago, I mentioned family and servants."

"With the exception of the name of the gentleman that was also present. An oversight, to be certain."

"As I remember it, the man's name was not provided by the vicar or Lady Victoria Grantham." That gaze narrowed even further.

"It is most curious that you would be interested in such a minor detail."

"It is most curious that you would neglect such a detail, given your reputation."

"As I said, the man's name was not given. Yet I did notice an accent. You must forgive me, Lady Forsythe. I only heard a comment as the service ended, and it was in French; foreign languages are not my strong point."

French! The man had spoken French with Victoria Grantham! Her London representative was well known about London and most certainly not French. That could mean that the man had accompanied her when she returned from France.

What was his part in this? Lover? An acquaintance for some other reason?

It was most interesting.

Burke had unwittingly provided me something that might be important in his haste to be as condescending as possible.

I then asked if there was anything peculiar or out of the ordinary about the funeral.

He gave me a look, that I very possibly did not want to know the meaning of.

"Since when do you have a fascination with funerals?" he asked. And another thought, "What of Lady Montgomery?"

It was a bit callous that his thoughts of my great aunt might be for her imminent departure, and his ability to have the story of the death of one of the most highly revered persons in the Empire for his collection. It would be quite a feather in his cap.

Not hardly, I thought. When and if that time came, which I was beginning to seriously doubt with each passing year, I would write about it myself and not leave it to someone who wanted only to further his ambitions.

I rose from the chair and tucked away the information he did not realize that he had provided. However, the most important question remained unanswered.

What did Victoria Grantham want?

To know her *real* family, according to that letter Aunt Antonia had received?

Or was it something else?

Brodie was waiting on the street adjacent to the Times offices. He assisted me up into the coach for my meeting with Victoria Grantham.

It made no sense to return to the office, then turn right around and make the ride back across London for the meeting.

"No blood let?" he commented.

"I thought about it," I replied. "However, he can be useful from time to time."

"Learned something important, did ye?"

"I don't know yet," I replied. "It seems there were very few mourners at the funeral for Lady Grantham, only two servants, which seemed odd to him for a member of the Grantham family. Victoria Grantham was there of course, and a man Burke didn't recognize as part of the family, with a French accent that he overheard."

"The young woman had been living in France," Brodie reminded me. And of course that seemed reasonable.

"He was given the assignment to cover the funeral due to Sir Grantham's long service in Parliament," I said, thoughtful.

"Yet, even though it was for his widow, Burke thought it particularly lacking for a member of a notable family. He was quite disappointed."

"It might have been due to the daughter living on the Continent," Brodie speculated. "With fewer connections remaining in London."

"Perhaps," I replied. Still, there was something about it that seemed very ... odd.

Waverly Park was small, more of a green with a handful of residences along each side that were of the late Georgian style. Waverly Place was one of the streets that circled the park of oak and birch trees, their branches bare of leaves with the season amid stands of juniper. Quite barren and gloomy in the gray afternoon, it reminded me of a book I'd read as a child—Sleepy Hollow. I half expected the headless horseman to come bounding down the dirt road that cut through the park.

Brodie had the driver pull up at the entrance to Grantham manor then handed me his umbrella.

"I'll wait at the entrance to the park."

I could have arranged for a driver to arrive at a specific time —perhaps no more than an hour would have been necessary as this was not a social call.

An hour would be more than enough time, I thought, for a

'brief' meeting to hopefully learn more about Victoria Grantham and the purpose of her contact.

Brodie gave instructions to the driver and they slowly circled round to the street, no doubt providing him a slow inspection of the manor and surrounding area—once a police inspector, I supposed, always one.

Our meeting was scheduled for two o'clock in the afternoon. I was thirty minutes early, most definitely not socially appropriate, yet it might work in my favor with an opportunity for me to make my observations once inside the manor.

I immediately noticed something unusual, as I reached the front entrance. There wasn't the usual black bunting about the door for a family in mourning that one usually found after a death.

Each to their own, I supposed. I certainly wouldn't care for wearing black, no matter who died.

As I twisted the doorbell lever to announce my arrival, I caught a movement along the hedgerow that lined the driveway at the far side of the manor.

A man in a long overcoat with top hat, moved quickly along the hedgerow. I heard the distinct sound of horses and a coach briefly lurched into view from alongside the manor where it had been waiting.

The coach lurched down the driveway out onto the street, then moved toward the main roadway with more speed than seemed necessary.

Most curious, I thought, as the man had obviously departed the manor from a different location and with some urgency.

An earlier appointment that had concluded? Or to avoid being seen?

The door at the entrance was abruptly opened by a small,

thin woman, who resembled a shriveled prune, dressed in a dark gray gown with a stiff white collar.

BRODIE

He saw the man as he left by way of a side entrance at the manor, then made his way to the coach that was partially hidden behind the hedgerow.

The man was well dressed, with a long coat and top hat, and carried a black bag, the professional sort Brodie had seen countless times on the streets of London.

He might have been a banker or possibly the lawyer the Grantham woman had hired. Except for his manner.

Brodie had encountered that manner countless time in his time with the MET—the quick look about to see if anyone had seen him, nervous as he reached the coach, then a destination hastily given as he quickly climbed inside.

The coach pulled away from the manor and rolled past where he waited, toward the high street beyond. Rental coach, No. 112, according to the city license attached at the rear, with a scar of some past mishap on the door, and a pair of mismatched horses—gray and black.

Who was the man? What was his reason for being there, and then departing in a hurry? With that instinct that had served him well, Brodie quickly decided and stepped down from the coach.

"Yer to wait for the lady," he told their driver, then set off at a run.

When he reached the high street, he found a cabman and climbed aboard.

"A coach just passed this way, No. 112 by the license, with a mismatched team. I need ye to follow, but at distance, and there'll be extra coin in it for ye."

"Right yer are, guv'ner," the driver called down as he maneuvered the rig into late afternoon traffic, then cut through an opening in the congestion until the coach came into view.

They followed at a distance as he requested, manor houses and squares in that part of London giving way to markets and shops. Then, onto Oxford Street as darkness closed in, and continued across London proper, past the Strand, then into Aldgate.

Here, the narrow streets ran one into the other, filled with tenements, shops with windows darkened at the end of day, and more than a tavern or two.

Brodie had his driver wait around the corner as the coach pulled up before a tenement building.

The man he'd seen leaving Grantham Manor stepped down, paid the fare, then took the steps down behind a wrought iron gate, and entered a part of the building below street level.

A light appeared in one of the basement windows.

"Wait here," Brodie told the cabman, and then crossed the street.

He reached the building, then moved toward the basement, and down the steps in that way that he'd learned a long time ago when he lived on the streets—quiet, careful, watchful.

He peered in the near window, smudged with grime from the street and the weather. Yet, clear enough to see what the man was about as he crossed that small room to a scarred wood cabinet and opened the door to reveal a small safe.

The man worked the combination, then the handle, and opened the safe. He then reached inside his coat and pulled out a thick envelope that he placed inside; something of value for safekeeping.

Money perhaps, Brodie speculated. If so, payment for what?

The safe door was quickly closed, then the scarred cabinet door as well. The black bag was tucked into a narrow closet. The man turned toward the entrance of the shabby flat. He put out the light, then opened the door.

Brodie flattened himself into the shadows as the man left that basement flat and crossed the street toward a tavern.

He watched as the man went inside, then went to the door of the flat. He pulled out the slender tool he always carried along with the revolver.

It was a simple matter, learned on the streets of Edinburgh as a lad. With patience and a careful hand, it was easily done, bypassing the 'wards' inside the lock on the door until he heard that sharp click as the bolt moved.

He pushed the door open.

Eight

THE WOMAN APPEARED to be the housekeeper, which seemed odd when I might have expected a doorman or butler with the status of the Grantham family.

I introduced myself and gave the reason I was calling on Victoria Grantham.

The woman appeared somewhat flustered.

"Yes, of course," she replied with what could only be called a cautious look about, then stepped back into the foyer so that I might enter.

She appeared uncertain what to do with me, then seemed to decide and asked me to follow her to a nearby room with a set of pocket doors. The room, lined with shelves of books, a large desk, and overstuffed wingback chairs, was obviously the library.

"Wait here. I will inform Lady Grantham that you have arrived."

It was obvious that my early arrival had caused some upset as she snapped the double doors shut behind her.

I had learned to be observant of people and my surroundings on my travels that exposed me to different places and cultures. And in working with Brodie, I had learned to observe both far more carefully.

A person's mannerisms, their hesitation or possible uneasiness, the twisting of hands, their eyes not meeting mine, often told far more than words. The woman's obvious agitation seemed most curious.

As for my surroundings, I had also learned from Brodie to quickly scan a room, looking for anything out of the ordinary, a cupboard or drawer left ajar, letters or other papers unattended on a desk or table, that might tell me something.

Of course, there was always the tell-tale bit of blood left behind or a body, always quite unsettling when first discovered. Yet as Brodie had pointed out more than once, I seemed to have an unusual fascination about such things, and had commented that most men might be put off by a woman who was not undone by the sight of blood.

I suppose my early experience with that as a child had prepared me for such things.

No blood here, I thought, with no small amount of cynicism as I made my inspection of the library while I waited for my meeting with Victoria Grantham.

Not that I had expected any. Yet, there was something ... a particular smell about the room.

A glance at the hearth revealed no residue of ash. There had obviously been no early morning fire. Yet, there was most definitely something there, as I circled toward the massive desk with those two wing-back chairs.

That impression disappeared as I rounded the far side of the desk to inspect the books that lined the shelves at the wall behind the desk.

One's choice in books often provided some insight into the

person who chose them, although I reminded myself that these books had undoubtedly been collected by Sir Grantham.

There were no works by Sir William Shakespeare or Mr. Dickens—the books here included several volumes of the House of Commons journal, and what appeared to be copies of the official records of Parliament. Much what I would have expected from a former member.

I passed behind the desk. It contained what one might expect to find—a pen on a carved wood stand, a desk calendar in a brass holder, the date almost a month past, a thick leather-edged desk pad, and what appeared to be correspondence from the bank. A voucher of some kind sat atop it, along with stationary bearing the Grantham crest.

As I continued my inspection and rounded the opposite side of the desk a piece of white cloth on the floor drew my attention.

I retrieved it and immediately caught that smell once again, though much stronger. It was slightly sweet, very much like mint, and familiar from one of our past inquiry cases when I had been injured and Mr. Brimley had tended my wound.

It was chloroform! And there were traces of pale marks on the cloth.

I had no opportunity to speculate further as there was a sound just beyond those double doors. I quickly tucked the cloth into the pocket of my coat, and turned as those doors opened and Victoria Grantham entered the library.

Once again, I was struck by the resemblance that had first drawn Lily's attention and then again at the art gallery reception. And the thought was there.

Was it possible that she was my sister, fathered through an affair by John Forsythe?

Her hair, somewhat darker than my own, was loose around

her shoulders, and she wore the same gown she had worn at the reception.

While the resemblance was a bit unsettling, there was something else about her ... that I had not noticed in the gas lights of the gallery.

"I was surprised when Mrs. Aldcott informed me that you had arrived early," she said with that faint accent I had noticed previously. "I hope that means there will be a pleasant beginning between us," she added as she swept into the library and indicated the two chairs across from the desk.

"I have asked for tea to be served," she said as I sat on one of the chairs and she took the one opposite.

We appraised one another as we waited for tea to arrive.

"I have been impressed by your endeavors," she commented. "Your travels, books, and your inquiry cases. Not what one expects for a lady."

She had previously spoken of it.

"I would like to travel as well," she added. There was a faint smile. "We might travel together perhaps, yes? And you could show me the places you have been," she suggested. "However, it would seem that your husband would not approve—Mr. Brodie, is it? A former detective with the Metropolitan Police, most unusual, I understand, and you are recently wed?"

Particularly well informed, I thought, and reminded her that she had requested the meeting to discuss the claim she had made.

"Yes, of course, and you can be most direct. I heard that about you as well. You are one who insists on details. It is an admirable quality when overseeing the vast affairs of the Montgomery family, considering Lady Montgomery's age."

Something she perhaps was not well informed about, it seemed, since I had no ambition for that. And I was not there to discuss my great aunt, the Montgomery family, or any of my great aunt's affairs.

"You are misinformed," I replied, to make everything perfectly clear. And I admit I also felt the instinctive need to protect my great aunt. "I have no involvement in her affairs, family, or otherwise. She is quite capable of taking care of those things."

There was that faint smile again. It wavered and was then gone.

"Yes, of course. She appears very capable. It would seem to run in the family."

"You have said that you want only to know your family," I reminded her. "That is something that could have happened before now," I pointed out. "Yet you are only now making that claim."

She rose from her chair, and appeared to steady herself with a hand on the chairback as she approached the hearth.

"You must surely understand how difficult this is. People are always eager for scandal." She turned. "My mother was ... very ill, and then her death. It was afterward that I found the letters. I didn't know what to think ... Yet, I felt compelled to reach out," she continued, hesitant.

"You seemed to be the one who would understand after losing *our* father in that most horrible way ..."

Our father? That seemed a bit presumptuous, I thought, and pushed back all those old feelings from long ago.

"If it is proven to be true." I was not willing to simply accept her claim, and she needed to know that.

"Of course it is true!" Once again there was an edge to her voice. "I have provided the letters and the documents." She laughed, a small sound that was quickly gone. "You have no doubt seen them!"

The conversation had become difficult. Yet I had not come here to argue the matter but in an attempt to learn more about her. Whether or not her claim was legitimate had yet to be determined.

"Surely you understand that this is an extremely important matter, not something to be treated lightly," I replied.

And certainly not something to be accepted because of a few letters and a document that was badly faded and almost illegible.

"Of course," she said, almost a whisper, as if deeply wounded.

What was I seeing in the obvious anger that quickly turned to unexpected laughter, then anger once more? Emotions at a very difficult time? The loss of her mother, and the discovery that the man she had always thought of as Father might not be her father?

I refused to argue the matter.

"Will you be remaining in London?" I asked, in an effort to ease the conversation and learn more about her.

"Of course!" she snapped, then seemed to collect herself as she pressed her fingers against the side of her head. She did seem to be in some discomfort.

"I apologize," she said haltingly. "I had hoped that we might be able to speak, however it is most difficult, as you can understand ..."

She seemed in some distress.

I came out of the chair and reached out to steady her as she most definitely appeared to be in some difficulty. From our meeting? Or was it something else?

"Should I call for your housekeeper?" I inquired. She seemed not at all well.

"No!" she replied quite firmly as she continued to press fingers against her right temple.

I took hold of her hand, to assist her.

"It's only a headache ..." she protested. "Yet, it seems that I must end our meeting. I apologize. We must meet again ..."

Those double doors suddenly opened and her housekeeper was there. Perhaps listening at the door?

That certainly seemed to be the case.

"See Lady Forsythe to the door," Victoria Grantham said in a shaky voice as she walked past me with some effort.

I watched as she made her way to the stairs with measured steps.

Suddenly taken with some malady? Or was it a very good performance?

It hardly seemed so. She had most definitely seemed to be in some discomfort.

"This way," the housekeeper reminded me.

Our meeting was most definitely at an end, as the housekeeper waited expectantly at the entrance to the library.

"Has she been ill?" I inquired as I followed her to the main entrance of the manor.

The epidemic of influenza that had seen us to Old Lodge in Scotland seemed to have mostly disappeared, yet I supposed there were still cases of it around the city.

"I could arrange for a physician to call on her," I suggested, and thought of Doctor Watson with the Agency.

"There is no need," she informed me with a glance toward that stairway.

We reached the foyer and she opened the door.

"Lady Forsythe ...?" she said as if there was something more she wanted to add.

"Yes?"

She glanced back at that stairway once more. Then appeared to change her mind.

"Take care with the weather."

I glanced past her. Victoria Grantham had reached the upper landing though with some effort, I thought, and was immediately joined by a man I had not seen as I arrived.

Was he the man Theodolphus Burke had seen at the funeral for Lady Anne Grantham? He most certainly had neither the demeanor nor the appearance of a servant.

"Good day," Mrs. Aldcott reminded me, somewhat sharply.

I tried to make sense of what had just taken place as I made my way down the front steps and then past the manor to the corner where I had left Brodie and the coach.

The coach was there, however Brodie was not.

"The gentleman took off in bit of a hurry," the driver said as he swung down from his seat atop the coach. "He did say as how I was to wait for you."

Anyone else might have been put off with being left. Yet I was not.

If Brodie had taken it upon himself to go off unexpectedly, it was for a good reason.

I thought of the man I had seen departing as we arrived earlier. Brodie had undoubtedly seen him as well. Nothing escaped his attention and I was fairly certain it was possible that was where he had gone.

I climbed into the coach and gave the driver the address of the office on the Strand.

It was very near evening by the time I reached the office due to congestion in the streets, and I discovered that Brodie had not yet returned.

Mr. Cavendish rolled out from the alcove in greeting.

"I've not seen him since you left earlier," he informed me. "Mr. Munro was here a while ago though and brought round a message. Said it was important." He pulled an envelope from inside his jacket and handed it to me. "Said you were to have it straight away."

The weather had taken a decided turn for the worse and I stepped under the overhang at the alcove to read it.

In spite of the thin light from the streetlamp, I immediately recognized the elegant handwriting on the envelope along with the Montgomery crest.

Mikaela dear,

It is imperative that we meet. Please come to Sussex Square when you receive this. I have news.

The note was simply signed with the first letter of her name as I had seen countless times, an elegant letter '*A.*'

She had news? That might mean anything. Yet my great aunt was not given to exaggeration or theatrics.

Contrary to what most persons thought, she was highly intelligent, observant, and could be a force to reckon with.

To quote HRH Prince Albert at the conclusion of a past inquiry case, he had expressed not only gratitude, but had made it quite clear that, contrary to what some people assumed, she could be quite formidable, and he was exceedingly grateful that she was a loyal subject of the Crown, and not the enemy.

She had simply replied, *Of course, Your Royal Highness.*

Now I asked Mr. Cavendish if Munro had said anything regarding the note when he delivered it, as he was often privy to my great aunt's affairs.

"No, miss. Only that it was important and I was to see that it was delivered to you."

I tucked the note into my bag. It did seem most important and I asked Mr. Cavendish to acquire a driver, as the man who had brought me to the Strand had promptly departed with his substantial fare.

"Mr. Brodie won't care for yer goin' off on yer own this time o' day," Mr. Cavendish reminded me.

He was correct in that, yet that note seemed most urgent.

"I will be quite all right," I assured him.

"Aye, and Mr. Brodie will have a conversation with me about that when he returns."

He waved down a coach across the way. The driver immediately swung around, pulled to a stop at the curb, and leapt down from his seat atop the coach.

"A moment if you please," Mr. Cavendish told him.

"That will cost you extra," the driver gruffly replied, not pleased with the delay. "I just passed up another fare."

Mr. Cavendish nodded to me and winked, then pressed two fingers against his lips and let out a sharp whistle.

It was somewhat more than a moment before Rupert came charging around the corner just beyond the smoke shop.

"Aye, there's a good lad," Mr. Cavendish said as the hound arrived, mud-splattered and with his usual smell of disgusting things I possibly didn't want to know about.

"Up with you, then, lad," Mr. Cavendish told him with a gesture at the inside of the coach.

"I don't take livestock, dogs, or drunkards," the driver growled.

"New to the Strand, are you?" Mr. Cavendish inquired. "The hound is a regular customer, well known by the other drivers with nary a complaint—an official guard dog so appointed by a member of the police."

The member of the MET was obviously Brodie. Although he didn't bother to mention that had ended some time ago.

And the rest of it? Exaggeration on a grand scale to be certain. However, admittedly, the hound had previously earned the unofficial role of protector, specifically when he saved my life.

I was not about to argue the point or explain to the driver.

"There will be extra coin in it for you," I informed him as I settled the argument by stepping past the driver and up into the coach so that we could be on our way.

There was more grumbling and I thought I heard a curse or two. The driver then latched the door, climbed back atop the coach and we were off.

Rupert grinned up at me from where he sat on floor of the coach.

Nine

THE RIDE to Sussex Square took the better part of an hour as the driver made our way through evening congestion of other coaches, wagons with the last delivery of the day, and the weather.

Upon our arrival I paid him an additional amount as promised.

"I never seen the like," he said in parting as Rupert ran up the steps to the main entrance.

I then joined the hound as the front door of the main entrance swung open and I was greeted by Mr. Symons, head butler and guardian of the door at Sussex Square.

He had been in my great aunt's employ for many years and had experienced not only her somewhat creative exploits, but mine as well.

"Good evening, miss." He cast a wary look down at Rupert.

Not that Mr. Symons disapproved of him, merely the chaos he caused when he had accompanied me in the past.

For his part, while the hound was usually well behaved

once inside the manor, he had a habit of exploring, which usually included a thorough inspection of the kitchens where food was most definitely a change from cast-off bones, a dead chicken, or an old boot found on the streets of the East End.

Not to mention that he had a habit of unsettling the servants. And then there were the gardens and the forest beyond, where something alive might be found. Most definitely paradise for a scavenger.

"Be on your way then," I told him.

I had no way of knowing whether or not he understood, of course, yet he immediately charged off through the *porte cochere* and around the corner, then disappeared.

Let the squirrels and birds be warned, I thought.

Mr. Symons did appear somewhat relieved. "Her ladyship is in the small drawing room."

"Is all well?" I inquired as I handed my umbrella and coat to a footman.

"Quite well, miss. Now that her ladyship has returned with the young miss."

"Returned?"

"They were out and about earlier today," he replied. "Taking care of business, as she explained."

In view of the weather that seemed a bit unusual. "I presume Mr. Munro accompanied them?"

"Miss Lily was with her, as she has become quite accomplished at maneuvering the motor carriage."

Oh, dear.

Aunt Antonia had acquired the motor carriage the year previous. Since then, she had practiced her skills, as she called it, motoring about the track she had installed on the green just beyond the gardens.

Practice had eventually included 'adventuring' across

London, usually with Mr. Munro, as a precaution against any mishaps or in the event she became disoriented. Each foray onto the streets of London had brought some concern with it on my part, as I imagined all sorts of catastrophes.

"It's quite all right," Lily had assured me, dressed in a motoring costume with a pair of goggles on that first 'excursion.' *"I carry a weapon, just in case we meet up with any rough sort."*

With that, she had brandished a flintlock revolver from the weapons display on the second-floor hall.

That had been less than reassuring. Yet, since then, Lily had become most proficient, due to Mr. Munro's lessons.

"It was either that or have her dispatch one of the servants by accident," he had explained, much to Brodie's amusement at the time.

"Aye, a bit of a resemblance," he had commented. I had ignored him.

Still, there was no ignoring the present situation or the urgency of that note.

My great aunt was not given to 'urgencies,' not even when I had taken myself off on one of my adventures a handful of years earlier with my Greek guide to the island of Crete, and she decided it was necessary to fetch me back to London as she put it—my first encounter with Brodie.

I thanked Mr. Symons and proceeded across the main hall to the 'small drawing room,' which was somewhat of a misnomer.

Sussex Square was a vast, sprawling fortress, the oldest parts very near eight hundred years old, from the time of the Conquest.

It had been re-built after some notable skirmishes with

enemies of the King at the walls—King William, that is, an ancestor of the Montgomery family.

It was re-built again over the centuries, and included the Georgian-style part of the manor that included a water tower that produced electricity—a recent addition that was much of an improvement over oil lanterns, indoor plumbing, and the dreaded telephone that Aunt Antonia was in the habit of cursing whenever it rang.

However, she was coming round on that one, and also did much appreciate the modern plumbing.

"Imagine," she had exclaimed more than once. "Indoor flush at the pull of the chain! Remarkable!"

After the death of both parents, Linnie and I had been raised in this somewhat odd but fascinating pile of stone and history. We had explored most of it, yet there were still parts we had not. Only recently I had ventured through the forest with Munro and discovered the Smugglers Gate.

I had always wondered if there was a dungeon. That was an exploration perhaps for Lily.

"Here you are, dear," Aunt Antonia greeted me as I reached the drawing room. "I thought you might have been kept overlong in your meeting with that nasty newspaper fellow ... or perhaps the Grantham woman," she added almost as an afterthought.

It always surprised me that she seemed to be very well informed. I might have asked her source for that information if not for something that immediately stopped me at the opening to the drawing room.

She was dressed in her motoring costume as she called it—a pair of tailored men's riding pants, matching jacket, with a turtleneck jumper, and knee-high boots. A pair of mud-splattered goggles lay on the side table where she stood with whisky glass in hand.

I should have expected it after Mr. Symons news of her adventure that day with Lily.

"There is such freedom in men's pants, don't you agree, Mikaela dear? Will you join me in a bit of whisky? The latest shipment is most excellent."

The latest shipment was always 'most excellent.'

She crossed the drawing room and handed me a tumbler.

I was still recovering from the sight of her costume when Lily arrived.

"Has she told ye?" she asked, quite excited. She was dressed much the same.

"Out and about in the city today?" I replied and took a sip, for courage I had once heard described. That certainly seemed that it might be the case.

"Just a bit of an outing," Aunt Antonia replied. "Quite tricky, navigating the streets in a downpour, but I thought the matter could be quite useful to our case."

Useful? Oh dear. And there was more.

"It came to me in a flash," she explained. "Something that could be most important," she explained. "Therefore, I placed a telephone call to Dickie, my banker. You do remember Sir Richard?"

I did and took another sip.

"I was put off by a clerk—simple young man. I doubt he can button his trousers by himself." She smiled.

"I then asked to speak with Sir Richard and explained to the clerk what it was that I wanted. I was informed that the information was a private matter and not provided to anyone outside the bank."

I pitied the poor clerk. He was obviously new, hadn't been forewarned, and had no idea who or what he was dealing with.

"That is when I decided that a visit to the bank was called for, and we set off."

"Munro should have accompanied you." I pointed out.

"He was off to see about the last delivery from Old Lodge. Not that he was needed. We made the trip quite efficiently."

"There was just the one incident," Lily added. "The man who tried to board the motor carriage."

Aunt Antonia waved it off. She obviously considered it of no consequence.

"A minor incident and Lily quickly dispatched the man."

When I looked over at Lily, she simply smiled. Another sip was required.

"Dickie was still in some meeting or another when we arrived." Aunt Antonia crossed the drawing room to one of the leather chairs in front of the hearth.

"Everyone was quite beside themselves when we entered the bank, particularly the clerk I had spoken with." She took up the tale. "We were immediately shown to a private office."

For the sake of everyone present, no doubt.

"I never saw the likes," Lily added. "As if the Queen had walked into the bank. Everyone rushing about, like when the ladies at the Church offered *free-ones* and customers crowded the place."

That momentarily halted the conversation. We both looked at her.

"Free ones?" Aunt Antonia was the first to recover. "I had no idea. How very enterprising."

It took me a moment to catch up. I did not ask for an explanation as the meaning was quite clear.

"That was when her ladyship told them what she wanted,

and we would wait until they provided the information," Lily explained. "Everything happened very quick after that."

I could only imagine.

"What information?" I managed to inquire.

Aunt Antonia motioned to Lily. "Another dram, Lily dear. If you please."

"I thought it could be useful to your inquiry case to have information about the financial situation of the Grantham estate," she explained as Lily poured. I held out my glass.

"Usually a private matter," I pointed out.

"Yes," she admitted. "However, there are ways ... And it did seem that the information could be important." She took another sip of whisky.

"I learned that Grantham had substantial debts, not unusual when one is a member of Parliament. They are not compensated, you know."

I didn't. However, there was more.

"They must rely on other means for their living." She set her glass on the side table.

"I had heard that Lady Anne had an inheritance upon the death of her father. Apparently that was substantially depleted over the years, and the debts were taken on as a matter of course, and for the usual things, including the education of the daughter; tutors, sent to France; and trips abroad later on."

That would have been Victoria Grantham.

"Not surprising there is a sizable loan from the bank." She poured another dram. "According to what I was told, the manor will have to be sold to pay the debts. It seems that Lady Anne had already made inquiries in that regard and had plans to retire to the country and live with a cousin or some other distant relation.

"Dreadful situation," she added. "As I have always said, one should never let a man handle one's money."

Words I had grown up with. I didn't bother to think about the influence all of this might have on Lily. I had survived quite nicely, and she would as well.

I did, however, think about the information Aunt Antonia had learned. The Grantham estate was deeply in debt. The only other support for some time had come from a family inheritance that was substantially depleted through the years, certainly not enough to live off. And Lady Anne had made the decision to retire to the country to live after the manor was sold to pay those debts.

It was a story that was all too familiar, including the situation Linnie and I had experienced as young children.

"What of Victoria Grantham?" I asked.

"Not without prospects," Aunt Antonia replied. "It does seem that Lady Anne has spent a great deal for the young woman's education over the years. She might find a position."

That did not seem likely of the young woman I had met with. That brought me back to those letters and documents.

Perhaps a way out of her financial difficulty? Most certainly, her claim might well be the means to provide that solution. If her claim was true.

"Now, you must tell me of your meeting with Victoria Grantham," Aunt Antonia insisted.

"It was very brief," I replied as I thought back to earlier that afternoon and tried to make sense of it.

"She seemed to be overcome by some malady and I was forced to leave."

"That is curious," Lily commented. "She was the one who insisted on the meeting."

I agreed. Instead of any answers, there were still only questions, and I thought of that cloth that I'd found in the library.

There had been no opportunity to examine it further after I received that message from my great aunt. I did wonder what that might tell us.

It was then that Mr. Symons announced that Brodie had arrived.

"Ah, Mr. Brodie," Aunt Antonia greeted him as he came into the drawing room. "You must join us. A dram, to take away the chill of the afternoon. Mikaela was just telling us about her meeting with Victoria Grantham."

That dark gaze met mine. I shook my head in a silent message that I would explain later, and handed him a tumbler of Old Lodge. He tossed back the contents.

"You were called away earlier," I commented.

"A minor matter ... for the agency," he replied.

It seemed there was a great deal to be discussed later.

"I see that ye and Miss Lily have been out and about, Your Grace."

"No need to stand on formalities, Brodie," she replied. "And you do seem to be in need of a bit of refreshment. Do see that your husband has another dram, Mikaela."

We passed the next hour as my great aunt shared once more about their adventure and what she had learned at the bank.

"Aye," Brodie replied with a look over to me. "The information could be important."

She insisted that we remain for early supper. We chose to leave afterward and made our excuses. Rupert had finally made an appearance, yet was not eager to accompany us.

Lily pleaded for him to remain. He seemed most content with that and had charged through the main hall to the distress of the household staff.

"Of course he must stay," Aunt Antonia announced. "Mr. Phipps has been complaining that we have a badger making a mess of the gardens. Perhaps Rupert can assist."

A badger—I wasn't at all certain which one might come out the better in a confrontation, although Rupert did have a great deal of experience with all sorts of dangerous encounters on the streets.

Much to Lily's delight, it was decided that he would remain, at least for the night.

"You will let me know if I can assist further," Aunt Antonia reminded us in parting, as Mr. Hastings, her coachman, arrived to take us back to the office. "The inquiry business is most exciting."

I had to admit that I cringed at the thought. I could only imagine the difficulties she might get herself into.

"She had a most excitin' day," Brodie commented as we departed.

"Do not encourage her," I replied. "It's one thing to make inquiries with her banker or Sir Laughton. It is quite another to have her off and about on the streets, looking for clues. She is quite taken with the idea and with no sense of caution."

"Sense of caution?" he replied, his expression amused in the light through the coach window as we passed a street lamp.

"Do not look at me that way."

"What way would that be?"

"You know very well," I replied.

The ride to the office on the Strand provided an opportunity to speak of things neither of us had shared earlier.

"It seems there is more to your visit with Miss Grantham than you shared with her ladyship," Brodie commented.

"And with you as well," I pointed out. "A matter for the Agency?"

An excuse, to be certain, as there were obviously things he'd learned that he chose not to discuss earlier.

"Aye."

Mr. Cavendish greeted us as we arrived.

"So, the filthy beggar has moved up with her ladyship," he commented drily regarding Rupert's stay-over.

"All well and good. The beast snores most pitiful, beg pardon, miss." Then added, "I think I'll take meself over to the Public House for a bit of ale, and get out of the weather."

That most usually included a stay-over with Miss Effie, who had a flat nearby. He would need to 'escort' her there after the 'Public House closed for the night.'

I climbed the steps after he set off across the street, pleased that he had 'a friend,' as he referred to Miss Effie.

I set my bag on the floor, then pulled that piece of white cloth from the pocket of my long coat.

The smell was still there, quite strong in spite of the fact that it was several hours since I discovered it. I laid it on Brodie's desk.

He arrived as well, closed the door and set the bolt, then removed his coat and hung it on the rack.

"Wot is this?" he asked as he noticed the cloth.

"'Something more' that I discovered in my meeting with Victoria Grantham."

He picked the cloth up and frowned, having obviously identified the scent. He looked over at me. "Chloroform?"

I went on to explain everything I had observed and sensed in that meeting with Victoria Grantham that had ended far too soon.

In addition to the smell of chloroform on that cloth, there was her manner, the responses that were cordial one moment, then quite agitated the next, along with the headache that came on and seemed quite dreadful. I had attempted to assist her and she had become quite angry.

There was something more.

"Yer instincts?" Brodie commented.

I had struggled with it on the ride earlier back to the office and since, that feeling that there was far more to the woman's story than we had yet learned. It seemed there might be a very strong motive to pursue her claim with the information Aunt Antonia had learned.

"What about that *'matter for the agency*?'" I asked regarding the excuse he had given earlier.

He then told me about the man we had both seen leaving the Grantham manor.

"Aldgate?" I replied with more than a little surprise.

It was a part of London far removed from Waverly Place, and initially might seem highly unlikely that Victoria Grantham would know anyone there. Yet, it appeared very much the situation.

Brodie had followed the man, then entered his flat after he departed and discovered exactly what he had placed in a safe. Whatever his connection was to Victoria Grantham, he had been well compensated.

"You might very well have been caught," I pointed out.

"The man was far more interested in the tavern on the corner, and Aldgate is not on the regular foot patrol of the MET."

He would know that of course.

"There has to be more to this."

What was the man about and the reason he had been at Waverly Manor? And now to learn that Victoria Grantham's situation was precarious financially? What did any of it mean?

Was it possible the woman's claim was false?

There was a part of me that wanted to believe it, in spite of the evidence she had provided ... in spite of that faint resemblance ... and in spite of her seemingly sincere reasons, that she only wanted to know her true family.

But was it something more?

"It's near midnight, lass," Brodie reminded me sometime later as I stared at the notes on the board.

"Come away for now. Ye willna find the answers tonight."

He was right of course. As much as I wanted—needed—to make sense of it. The solution wasn't there. Yet.

$$Ten$$

I WAKENED several times through the night, and each time Brodie was there—with his solid strength and gentle words whispered in Scots that persuaded me back to sleep. And I dreamed.

I was a child again, and there was the sound of the gunshot at the stables at our country home. Pigeons scattered into the sky and clouds of dust filled the air as I ran into the stables, then suddenly stopped at the sight of my father's body, and the blood.

In my dream, I called out, but there was no answer. There was only the sound one of the horses made in their stalls, and then the frantic howl of the hounds in their kennels ...

I sat up in the bed in the room adjacent to the office. It was empty beside me.

There were voices, and a persistent scratching sound at the door that had been closed between the rooms.

I recognized Brodie's accent, and then a response, also with that Scots accent—Munro. And the faint scratching sound could only be the hound.

I rose, splashed water on my face from the basin and dressed, then opened the door.

"Rude bloody beast!" Munro commented. "I threatened him earlier, but he set up such a stramash on the street below that I brought him up to the office. Pardon, miss."

"Not to worry. I overslept," if it could be called that, as I scratched the 'rude, bloody beast' about the ears. He now seemed most content, except for the fierce wagging of his tail.

Brodie frowned where he sat at the desk.

"There's coffee and breakfast on the stove, Mr. Cavendish brought earlier."

I wasn't certain whether the frown, handsome as it was with that dark beard around it, was about the breakfast or myself.

Admittedly, I had been somewhat taken aback at my appearance in the mirror above the washbasin. Dark circles were not what most women hoped to present to the world.

I had brought my hair into some order with a ribbon and combs. That would have to do at present, as I made my way to the stove and coffee. Very strong coffee. It was much appreciated.

"Better?" Brodie inquired as I crossed the office to the chair at the desk that now occupied the back wall of the office, along with the portable typewriter that he had purchased for me.

Wonderful invention that, and made typing up our reports, not to mention my latest work in progress, far easier than needing to return to the townhouse each time. Most thoughtful.

Munro stood. "I'll be going now, and I'll see to that matter," he told Brodie.

"Take care not to be discovered," Brodie cautioned. "We dinna know what the man is about."

Munro nodded. "Careful as a thief in the night."

With a lick to my hand the hound followed him out the door. So much for being the favorite person in the room.

"That did seem somewhat ominous," I commented as I sat in the chair opposite Brodie's desk.

"Necessary, as ye well know, in places where one doesn't want to be seen."

"Aldgate?"

"He makes frequent trips about the city on business for her ladyship. I've asked him to inquire about the man I followed."

I was not surprised.

I refilled my cup then went to the blackboard.

Motive, means, opportunity. It was always there, as I had learned from Brodie. The question now?

What was Victoria Grantham's motive?

There was obviously financial difficulty, as my great aunt had learned.

The means?

It would seem the letters and that somewhat damaged document provided the means for her claim.

And the opportunity? That was not yet clear, as she had already made the claim.

And what about the chloroform on that piece of cloth?

I wanted to speak with Mr. Brimley about that. He might be able to offer some insight other than my brief experience with it previously.

The telephone rang, a sharp, jangling sound that was somehow more irritating than usual, no doubt due to little sleep the night before.

At the moment, I was inclined to agree with my great aunt, and cursed the bloody thing.

In the interest of preventing it being yanked from the desk

and thrown across the room, Brodie picked up the handpiece. How was it that he could be so very cordial after little sleep?

Oh, yes, I reminded myself. It had to be that previous experience as an inspector with the MET, and his somewhat criminal life on the street before that.

I took another sip of coffee, then caught a bit of conversation. The call was from James Warren, my sister's husband. Also known as my publisher.

However, the call was not regarding that ever-present question, *when would I be delivering my next book.*

It was about another matter that he wished to discuss at his office, not over the telephone. It seemed quite serious.

Brodie handed me the earpiece. My first thought was for Linnie.

Was there some difficulty with the pregnancy? He assured me that was not the situation, but still insisted that we meet.

We agreed to meet at ten o'clock.

"I'll go with ye," Brodie announced.

James's office was very near Mayfair. There was just enough time for us to return to the townhouse so that I might change into fresh clothes, as my gown was thoroughly stained with mud from the day before.

Even though James had reassured me that Linnie was quite well, I still worried as we returned to the townhouse and I changed clothes, then on the cab ride to his office. It was not like him to be so very serious, or secretive.

We arrived at the appointed time, and Brodie escorted me inside the two-story Georgian building that had once been a residence and was now the office for Warren & Co. Publishers.

I had been here countless times and we were greeted by

Mrs. Burton, who had read all of my novels and had been a fan from that first adventure. She smiled warmly. No clue there as to that early morning call from my brother-in-law.

"Mr. Warren has been expecting you." She escorted us to his office.

He rose from behind his desk as we arrived and thanked Mrs. Burton. He indicated the chairs across from his desk, although he remained standing, and waited until she had gone.

"I do appreciate your meeting me on such short notice."

"The matter seemed important," Brodie replied.

James nodded. "It's regarding the recent claim made by Victoria Grantham."

I exchanged a look with Brodie. While James and Linnie were both aware of the situation, there had been no reason to include them as far as our inquiries were concerned.

In fact, I deliberately chose *not* to include them, other than to ask him to let me know if the woman made any effort to contact them. I did not want Linnie upset in any way by the situation.

"She has contacted you?"

"In a matter of speaking," he replied, then retrieved a wrapped bundle from a drawer in his desk and dropped it onto the desktop with obvious irritation.

"I received this two days ago by courier, and thought nothing of it until I had the time to open it yesterday. As you well know, Mikaela, I receive numerous submissions for publication, including yours. But this ..." he made a gesture toward the bundle which appeared to be a manuscript. "I found it extremely disturbing. You will no doubt recognize the author."

I approached the desk and retrieved the manuscript.

"Written by Lady Victoria Forsythe."

"I did read the first few chapters," James continued,

"although I said nothing about it to Linnie. You will find it quite alarming. According to the woman's letter that accompanied it, it is meant to be fiction. Yet what she has written ... is as if she has written about Emma Fortescue's first adventure." He looked at me. "I found it to be most disturbing.

"I have no intention of publishing it," he assured me. "You may read it, of course." He looked over at Brodie.

"I know that you are making inquiries about the woman's claim. Perhaps it will provide some insight." He then added, "And I urge you to take great care with your inquiries."

"It does seem there may be cause for concern," Brodie replied. "Particularly when the woman learns you will not be publishing the book."

By the expression that suddenly appeared, James had obviously not considered that.

"I see your point." He was thoughtful. "I can send round a note that it will be some time before I will be able to include it into our publishing schedule. That should provide time for you to resolve the matter of who the woman is."

That was quite brave of him. Still ...

"Linnie doesn't know anything about this?"

"No. I stayed here at the office to read it. That seemed to be advisable under the circumstances."

I looked over at Brodie. He knew perhaps better than anyone, other than Aunt Antonia, that I would do anything to protect my sister, and in fact had when I first contacted him. We exchanged a look.

"Aye, I know someone who can be trusted to protect ye, if I ask it. He and his people will be discreet ... he prefers it that way. But he's not the usual sort ye would find in this part of London. I would trust him with Mikaela's life."

"Good heavens! You're suggesting that we might be in some danger?"

"It must be considered," Brodie replied.

I thought of the people he knew from his time with the MET; however, his description could mean only one person whom I had previously met on a case.

"Very well," James agreed. "What should I tell Linnie?"

"Ye tell her nothing. Neither of ye will know his men are about. It's best that way."

"Mr. Brown?" I questioned as we left James's office with that manuscript written by Victoria Grantham.

I had read no further than the title page. I would read it later for anything that might tell us about her and her claim. As I knew well enough, it was not unusual for an author to include a great deal about themselves.

As for Mr. Brown, he was most certainly not the sort to be found on the streets of Mayfair.

"Ye can trust him to protect both yer sister and James," Brodie replied. "I'll get word to him."

It was true that Mr. Brown had proven himself to be a man of his word, as well as resourceful. Yet, there was the small matter of his reputation as a thief, smuggler, and some nasty business about certain people who simply disappeared when they attempted to cheat him out of a cargo while doing 'business.'

Still Munro trusted him. As for myself ...

"It's rumored that he has committed murder," I reminded him on that ride back across the city, and a meeting I hoped to have with Mr. Brimley regarding the chloroform on that piece of cloth.

"The same could be said of myself, lass. I wasn't always with the Metropolitan."

There was that. Which I accepted quite simply because I knew him, and he had come highly recommended by my great aunt—a man I could trust. And I did.

"There is that other part of it about Brown," he added.

"What part?"

"The man is most fond of ye."

"Fond?" I remarked with more than a little surprise. "As in ...?"

That smile across the inside of the coach, always a bit devilish.

"He's never before known a lady who can speak four languages, prefers whisky, shoots a revolver, and curses better than himself."

He leaned forward and took my hand, then kissed the palm. The sort of simple gesture that ... made my toes curl.

"I suspect ye have him under a spell."

I burst out laughing at the ridiculous notion.

"And myself as well, lass."

Mr. Brimley's assistant, Sara, greeted us when we arrived at his shop. We were told that he was presently conducting an experiment.

"It was after ye left the other day, about the lemon juice ..." she explained when there was suddenly an excited shouted from the back of the shop.

"Success! I did it!"

Mr. Brimley emerged from the back of the shop, quite a

sight to be certain. He wore a long leather apron, leather gloves, and goggles, and waved a piece of paper about.

He stopped and blinked when saw us, then pushed the goggles back.

"You are responsible," he announced in that somewhat confusing manner. "You must come and see the results."

With that, he spun around and charged into the back of the shop once more.

Brodie and I followed.

"I do hope he is not about to explode the place," I commented.

We found him at one of his *work stations*, as he called them, with an array of bottles, brushes, and the paper he'd been waving at us, along with the distinct smell of lemon.

"You started me thinking, Miss Forsythe ... Most extraordinary!"

He looked up as he carefully held that piece of paper over a gas burner that he used for sterilizing instruments, and a meal when he remembered to eat.

"Watch carefully now," he told us.

The paper gradually heated then turned brown about the edges as letters slowly began to emerge on the paper with a message, the current date—30 November 1892!

"A hidden message," he announced, then seized another piece of paper from the countertop. Across the paper was a note—*To Whom It May Concern*.

He repeated the steps, holding the paper with the note over the burners. Eventually the date 29 November 1892 emerged.

"It works, the exact opposite of what I attempted when you brought that document to me." He was as excited as a child at Christmas.

"The message is painted with the lemon juice. I then allow

it to dry, and it's invisible, revealed only when the paper is heated!"

It was quite extraordinary.

"Secret messages," I commented.

"Most interesting," Brodie added.

Mr. Brimley looked up. "I think you are not here to discuss my little experiment."

"I need your assistance," I replied.

"What might that be, Miss Forsythe?"

"I need to know more about chloroform."

He indicated for us to follow him to the small office that was hardly more than a closet at the back of the shop. An adjacent storage room was used from time to time as a small recovery room after one of our cases.

He sat behind the desk and poured a dark liquid from a beaker.

"Tea—the girl keeps it warm for me. Please have a seat."

I took the chair across from him.

"I know that it is used prior to surgery, for pain," I said. "I need to know if there are symptoms one might experience afterward."

"Most interesting," he commented. "I trust not for yourself. Perhaps one of your inquiry cases.

"Some people might experience changes in their manner," he continued. "They might become easily angered, perhaps even have hallucinations, wild imaginings of their surroundings, but most usually that would be with recurring use. It eventually wears off, as you well know."

Did that describe what I had seen in Victoria Grantham?

"Might a person be unsteady and have trouble walking?"

"Of course, if they attempted to go about their usual way right afterward."

It did seem as if that might have been what I had seen during my visit with Victoria Grantham. I retrieved the cloth I had found from my bag and laid it on the desk.

"What can you tell me about this?"

Mr. Brimley picked up the cloth and carefully examined it.

"A fine piece of linen, stained with those few marks, and ..." he smelled it. "With the faint smell of chloroform."

"What about the marks?" Brodie asked. "Can ye identify them?"

"On the shelf in the storeroom," he replied. "There is a large jar of water." He smiled. "If you please, Mr. Brodie."

Brodie retrieved the jar and set it on the desk.

"For my experiments, quite pure. Not the muck that comes through pipes compliments of the City of London." He grinned, then removed the lid and poured a portion in a glass bowl. He resealed the jar, then dipped the cloth into the bowl of water.

"Ah, there it is," he announced as the stains darkened. "Blood to be certain, I've seen my share. And chloroform as well, the smell quite strong now."

It was late afternoon when we left his shop. From what we had learned it did seem very likely that Victoria Grantham had been experiencing possible effects from the chloroform on the cloth that I had discovered.

But for what reason? And the traces of blood that Mr. Brimley was able to identify? Was it her blood?

I had not seen any injury.

Brodie asked Mr. Cavendish to put out the word on the street that he wanted to meet with Mr. Brown, while I climbed the stairs to the office. And we waited.

While we waited, I added what we had learned to the blackboard, including that disturbing information from my brother-in-law.

It was well into the evening when the service bell sounded on the landing.

Mr. Brown had arrived and filled the entrance to the office.

He was as I remembered him from our last encounter, very near the same height as Brodie, but with a thicker frame, heavily muscled with a roll of flesh at the back of his neck below the rim of his cap.

He wore the clothes of a street or dock worker with a heavy worsted coat, corduroy pants, a blue cotton shirt, with a wool scarf and boots.

He had a scar that ran the length of his face from his left eye to his chin, and when he smiled, as now, it revealed several teeth were missing.

"Brodie," he said by way of greeting, then turned to me. "And the lovely lady, with the opportunity to warm meself before a warm fire of a cold night. What could it be, I asked meself, that Angus Brodie puts the word out on the street most urgent?"

Eleven

BRODIE POURED two tumblers of my great aunt's whisky and pushed one across his desk to Mr. Brown. I had no desire to join the conversation and sat apart at my desk.

Brodie explained that we had come across a disturbing situation while investigating our present case, the possible danger to someone.

Brown watched him through narrowed eyes. "What is it that you want?"

"Protection for the people involved until we can solve the case."

"Why call on me? Call on your friends at the MET."

"This is not for the MET," Brodie replied. "It would draw attention and perhaps place others in danger. And I need someone I can trust."

Brown laughed. "You and me, we go round and round. You do me a favor and then I owe you a favor. Which is it now, I forget?"

"You remember, well enough. Yer man, Darby."

"Darby?" Brown repeated.

I thought he might argue the matter.

"Aye, Darby," he said then. "A reckless fool, but one that I need. And my gratitude to you for it."

Whatever it was, it was very likely that I did not want to know how it had involved Brodie.

"I want reliable men who will stay out of sight and not a word to anyone of it."

Brown nodded. "I have three men that will do. Who is the person to be protected?"

Brodie provide him the information that included James's and Linnie's names, the location of their residence, and James's office.

"Not the Queen herself?" Mr. Brown retorted with some humor.

"My sister and her husband," I informed him, interrupting what seemed to me unnecessary banter.

Brown turned to me. "Yer sister, is it? It's a wonder you don't have a pistol and protect her yerself."

He had no way of knowing how close to the mark he had come.

"Ye will provide yer men and give them instructions as I have given them to ye?" Brodie reminded him.

"Aye, I will." Brown turned back to him. "But this evens the score."

Brodie nodded his agreement.

Brown tossed back the last of the whisky, then stood to leave.

"I'll have Darby and two men there in the morning. Since it's his arse you saved, he's beholden to you and will do as ye ask. He can be trusted."

I had heard that before, yet from someone whom I trusted.

He turned to me then with that smile that was not quite a smile. A leer perhaps?

"Always a pleasure, Lady Forsythe."

His entirely, I thought, and simply nodded.

"How can you be certain that you can trust him in this?" I asked after Mr. Brown left.

Brodie pulled me against him, "Because I know things."

I leaned back and looked up at him. "What sort of things?"

"Not for you to know, lass."

Which of course told me absolutely nothing, and at the same time more than I perhaps wanted to know.

In spite of the late hour and little sleep the night before, I wanted to read the manuscript my brother-in-law had given me, apparently written by Victoria Grantham.

Authors wrote from their own experiences. I thought of Dickens with poverty in the East End; Arthur Conan Doyle, an author I had heard a great deal of; and certainly the woman who had inspired me—Mary Wollstonecraft.

My adventures with Emma Fortescue as my protagonist came from my own experiences. That included new adventures in crime solving, based thinly on our inquiry cases. That Victoria Grantham had chosen to write a book did seem quite bizarre.

My brother-in-law had read several chapters. What had she written that had caused such concern? And what might it tell us?

I turned over the first page with her name on it, then the first page of the manuscript. The first line of that first paragraph stopped me:

"She had been raised in privilege. But everything ended that day.'

A coldness I had not experienced in a very long time crept over me as I stared at the words. And there was anger all over again. It was the first line of my first Emma novel, and as I continued to read, entire scenes had been lifted and put into her novel.

I had taken many things from my own life and given them to Emma's character. But this ...? It was plagiarism, in the least. But for what reason? A cold chill ran through me.

"What is it?" Brodie asked.

I looked up and found that dark gaze watching me, worry lines about the frown that was there.

I shook my head and forced myself to continue, reading through the introduction from the author, about the child who found her father dead, she and her younger sister orphaned, and the woman who had taken them in. And then the novel itself.

Page by page, chapter after chapter, it was as if I was reading what I had written all over again, the adventures identical.

My work written as if it was *hers*!

Brodie was there.

Not a ghost, but very real with concern in that dark gaze, and quiet strength.

"Enough, come away, lass."

I wasn't aware that I pushed away from my desk, nor did I notice the small things that usually happened of an evening when we stayed over—Brodie setting the bolt at the door, extra coal that he put in the stove, the light turned off as he led me to the adjacent room.

I was only aware of his warmth and that strength that wrapped around me. And then quite impossibly, I fell asleep.

•   •   •

No ghost of the past, I woke to the usual morning sounds after staying over at the office the night before—the iron grate on the stove, the sound of the coffee pot set atop, a window shade opened, and the scrape of a chair on the wood floor as Brodie went to his desk.

It was still there, of course, everything that Victoria Grantham had written, disturbing and sad.

I splashed cold water on my face, dressed, then stepped into the outer office as I had dozens of times. The manuscript was there on the desk before him. I struggled between tears and laughter as reading was not his finest accomplishment.

He looked up. He understood in a way that few could. It was there in the sadness in those dark eyes.

"I want to go to Compiegne," I announced, where Victoria Grantham supposedly was born.

"It is the only way to know for certain."

There was no argument against it, no attempt to talk me out of it with winter coming on, no discussion that we should continue our inquiries here with what we knew. There was only that one word that meant more to me than he could possibly know.

"Aye, I knew ye would not be satisfied until ye did. But ye'll not go alone."

In spite of everything, I smiled to myself, as we boarded the cross-channel ferry after our arrival in Dover. While I had a great deal of experience with ocean travel from my adventures abroad, Brodie was most definitely not the sea-faring sort.

We had been warned that trip might be rough, white caps churning the water of the channel. There was only a brief muttered curse as we boarded the ferry with dozens of other passengers.

"What is it?" Brodie asked as I hesitated at the entrance to the passenger cabin.

It was a moment before I replied as I searched the faces of our fellow passengers, and discovered ...

"I thought I saw someone ..." I shook my head. "I'm certain that it's nothing." I continued into the cabin as a heavy rain began.

To say the crossing was rough was a mild understatement, although he did bear up quite well. There was only a faint tinge of green around his mouth as we arrived at the Port of Calais, then found a driver to take us to the rail station.

Unlike a previous trip, we had only an hour's wait until the train to Paris arrived.

However, we would not be traveling the full distance. Compiegne, in the Oise department, was north of Paris on the route from Calais, reached by way of a change at Creil.

In spite of the fact that the train from Calais was an express, we would be arriving at Creil well into the evening and would be forced to remain until the following morning before continuing on to Compiegne.

I could only wonder what we might find there. Things changed over time, and the care home where Anne Grantham had gone to have her child might no longer exist.

Yet, there would be the office of the local prefect, and undoubtedly someone who would be able to direct us to the office where that record of birth had been issued.

I glanced over at Brodie, seated across from me in the rail car. Several passengers dozed in the warmth of the heated car after that cold crossing, and it was quiet except for an occasional murmur of voices.

"Do you believe in ghosts?" I asked him.

I don't exactly know the reason it was important for me to know. Perhaps a way of understanding what was happening now, from someone I trusted.

He had been watching out the side window, absorbed in his own thoughts. That dark gaze met mine.

"*Taibhsean*," he softly replied in Scots Gaelic, thoughtful. "There those who believe in such things, spirits, and the like. I am not a religious person as ye well know, still ..." he hesitated, then continued.

"There have been times in the past when it seemed that I felt my mother's presence, her hand on my shoulder in that way she had, a word she often said, warning me about something I was doing. Or perhaps only wishful thinking, ye ken?"

Ghosts of the past.

"And perhaps," he suggested, "her spirit saw to it that I rescued ye that day on that Greek island."

Rescued me, indeed. The topic of discussion on more than one occasion, as to precisely who had rescued whom. Still, as Sir William Shakespeare had once written, '*Oh, what a falling off was there.*'"

We departed the train at Creil and then went by local driver to an inn.

We were both tired, yet quite amazingly I was hungry.

"England could be invaded, and ye would want supper first," Brodie pointed out.

I pointed out that our previous meal had been supper at Sussex Square. I did not consider a biscuit that morning from the Public House to be a meal.

We were served a hearty soup with large pieces of meat, potatoes, and leeks, and fresh croissants warm from the oven at the inn.

He managed quite well to consume two bowls of soup and a half dozen of the croissants. I restrained myself from commenting the same to him.

We retired to our room afterward, and I took out my notebook that contained notes I had made before leaving London.

A fire had been lit when we first arrived and had burned low. Brodie added more wood on the hearth as a chill set in.

"You should be prepared—there is always the possibility we will find nothing," he reminded me as he set the screen before the fire.

He was right, of course. Not everything we pursued in past inquiries had brought results, yet those instances had often led to something that had. I had learned that particularly well in that first case that had involved my sister.

I undressed for bed. However, as I had discovered when previously traveling with Brodie other than to Old Lodge in Scotland, he chose to remove only his boots. A habit from the streets, he had once explained, if there should be the need to quickly leave.

We lay in the room with only the glow of the light from the hearth. His shoulder was solid and warm under my cheek.

I was safe from the ghosts of the past, for now.

We rose early in order to make the morning train to Compiegne. We arrived in just over an hour.

The rail station was at the edge of the town, the main station like many I had seen before, with the two-story main station that included an open platform for trains arriving from Paris, and a smaller station for departure farther to the north.

The main station was crowded with arriving passengers,

umbrellas opened against the rain that had followed us from Creil.

There was that variety of languages commonly found in towns and cities across the Continent, as people moved past to find transportation into the city or another connection, while others crowded the ticket counters seeking the schedule for the next train to Paris.

"Have ye been here before?" Brodie asked.

I hadn't, yet it should be easy enough to find information about the home where Anne Grantham had gone all those years before. If it was still there. After more than twenty years, it might have ceased to exist. Although the need for such places had not changed from what I had seen in the East End of London.

I was hopeful that we might learn something as we passed through the rail station and found a driver to take us into the city.

The ride was not far, large buildings like boxes in the style of the Second Empire, with mansard roofs and ornate ironwork along the main thoroughfare, and centuries-old buildings in the Gothic style in contrast with the spires of a cathedral rising over the city.

The driver delivered us to a city square before the Hotel de Compiegne in that same style of the Second Empire.

The decision to come to Compiegne had been quickly made. There had been no opportunity to exchange currency before leaving and I had only a few francs left from an earlier trip over on another case. It was enough to pay the driver's fare.

As I had discovered in my travels, the hotel might be able to exchange currency for us, as well as provide information where we might find the home where Anne Grantham had gone to await the birth of her child years earlier.

"Aye," Brodie agreed. "And send a telegram to London."

The hotel concierge at the desk where guests arrived informed us that they accepted most currencies, including English pounds, and could make that exchange. In addition, they could also provide telegram service when Brodie asked. As we knew well, there was not yet direct telephone connection to London.

I then inquired about the home where Anne Grantham had come to have her child. There was a faint look of surprise from the clerk who spoke English quite well.

"*Oui, madame.*" He responded that it was some distance north of the city, but could be reached by coach.

We had no way of knowing how long we might need to remain in Compiegne to find the information we were looking for. In addition, there were only a handful of trains through the day that made the return trip to Calais, and none at night.

It was already near midday and Brodie thought it best that we take a room at the hotel. That would provide us with a coach for the trip north of the city.

Brodie went to send his telegram to Munro while arrangements were made for a driver.

Neither of us had eaten that morning before leaving Creil. As the hotel restaurant was not yet open for luncheon, the concierge recommended a café across the square.

I was familiar with French cafés and the preference for taking a meal at an outside table. However, the weather was cold with a light rain and we chose to eat inside.

I translated the handful of items available written on a board as we entered.

"Soup?" Brodie commented, and not in a complimentary manner. This from a man who was once forced to live on little more as a child. That perhaps explained his disdain for French food that frequently included soup.

Still, having not eaten since the previous evening I was inclined to agree. We took a nearby table and I ordered a baguette of bread with sliced ham and cheese, and of course ... wine.

We returned to the hotel afterward and were directed to the *porte cochere* at a side entrance where we found a driver waiting, and no small amount of hope for we might learn as we climbed aboard.

The ride took us through the city business district, then crossed the river to the older part of Compiegne. Here, modest brick houses with slate roofs lined the dirt thoroughfare of a modest village at the edge of the city.

The driver called down and informed us that '*La Maison de Anges,*' the House of Angels, was just beyond.

Brodie had prepared me that we might find nothing; still I hoped there might be some record of Anne Grantham's stay.

The coach eventually turned up a narrow cart path, then pulled around before a low, pink sandstone building. The spire of the Church of St. Jacques was visible nearby through the misty rain.

In spite of the fact that I had not been to Compiegne before, I was familiar with stories of Joan of Arc.

It was where she had been captured at prayers more than four hundred years earlier. She was then taken to Rouen, tried for witchcraft before an English court, of all things, then burned at the stake.

"The verdict was changed afterward," I explained to Brodie. I suspected that hardly made a difference to her.

Brodie asked the driver to wait. We then followed the path that led to the entrance of the large building that reminded me of a convent. That impression was not misplaced as we were met by a nun who answered the bell at the door.

I explained in French the reason we had come, regarding information about a child that was born there several years before, and added that it was a family matter.

We were asked to wait and she went to speak with someone who might be able to help us.

Brodie had been particularly silent. That might have been explained by the fact that the nun had spoken only French. Yet the expression on his face suggested more.

"It's been a long time since I was in such a place," he made the excuse.

"Concerned about your sins?"

The more I had learned about him since that first inquiry case, I had discovered there were dark places in his past, and people with equally dark reputations.

"I would vouch for your soul," I whispered as the nun returned and we were shown to a room that contained shelves lined with books, a crucifix on the wall, and the woman who sat at a desk.

"You must understand what you ask is unusual," the Reverend Mother said in heavily accented English as we sat across from her.

"We provide sanctuary for women who find themselves ... in difficult situations. Some come here to have their child, then return home. Some of the children ..." Her voice softened. "We try to find homes for those whose mothers cannot care for them, or choose not to."

I explained that we were looking for information about a woman who would have come there approximately twenty years ago and explained that the child was now a grown woman who claimed to be a relative. I then showed her the document

Victoria Grantham had provided with that faded name at the bottom.

"Sister Sandrine," she commented. "Sadly, she is no longer with us."

"Do you have records for the women who come here?" I asked. "Something that would show the mother's name, and possibly the father's name as well?"

"We have records of the women and girls who come to us, but we do not require the name of the father unless it is freely given. You must understand that privacy and sanctuary are the reasons women come here, and it is part of what we do."

She rang a bell and a young woman appeared. She was not dressed as a nun. Perhaps she was from the village we had passed through, or possibly someone who sought sanctuary there.

There was a brief exchange in French as the Reverend Mother requested to see a record book from the same date as the document I had provided.

"You speak French," the Reverend Mother commented as we waited. "You are perhaps familiar with the Church of St. Jacques?" She mentioned the church we had seen as we arrived.

I replied that I was. Nothing more was said as we waited.

The young woman eventually returned with a book that looked very much like a ledger.

Reverend Mother thanked her, then opened it on the desk. She turned several pages and I thought of the names there and the women who had come here, including Anne Grantham. She then stopped and scanned several entries. She looked up.

"It is here. The young woman you speak of was here for several months, then delivered of a daughter. According to what is here, she left with the child. No name for the father was written."

We had come there hoping to find the answer to the questions about Victoria Grantham, although I knew that Brodie was right. That the answer might not be here.

I showed her the other document that appeared to be a copy of an official document with that entry that was no longer legible.

"This is a copy, but can you tell me who would have provided the original document?"

She frowned. "It would seem that the mother of the child chose to have the birth registered."

I asked where that might have taken place.

"It is possible the original document is at the Hôtel de Ville, in Compiegne. They have records of marriages, births, and deaths. They may be able to help you." She rose as we stood to leave.

"I pray that you find what you are looking for."

I had only English pounds left, but made a donation to the home as we left.

Our driver had waited. Brodie asked him to take us to the Hôtel de Ville.

"Hotel?" Brodie repeated as we entered the coach.

I explained that it was a typical French term. Hôtel de Ville, or the town hall, where public records were kept.

It was late afternoon when we returned to the city.

The Town Hall was an impressive Gothic structure several hundred years old that I had glimpsed when we first arrived in Compiegne, with conical towers at each corner, and an enormous clock at the base of a central spire that was wrapped in low clouds.

It was very near the hotel where we had made arrangements earlier for the night, and there seemed no reason for our driver to wait. He tipped his cap, then left to return to the hotel.

According to the signage on the glass door at the entrance there was still an hour before the building was closed for the day.

Brodie opened the door and we entered the building, hardly a hotel in the usual manner, but an old building typical of many in Paris that had been designated as the Town Hall for the city of Compiegne.

I approached a clerk behind a desk and explained what we were looking for. He directed us to the department of records on the second floor, with a reminder that the building closed for the day at five o'clock. That was one thing I had learned the French people were very punctual about—closing time.

We reached the second floor. A long counter filled the center of the floor with wooden shelves at least ten feet tall behind it, very much like a library.

I showed the copy of that old document to the clerk and again explained the reason we were there—to see the original document with the hope of reading the names that had been entered.

He nodded and explained that it should be easy to find the document as the date of the copy was recent compared to far older records that were kept.

I glanced at a clock on the wall when it seemed he was gone for some time. He eventually returned.

"I am sorry, *madame*. I was not able to find the original document. It would seem to have been misplaced."

Misplaced? Surely he was mistaken.

"Did you search thoroughly?"

"*Oui*, the birth documents for that date and several others both before and after the date. I could not find it."

"Is it possible that someone else might have asked to see it?"

There was another thought that came. "Or that it was removed? Would there be a record of that?"

"Removed? No, *madame*. We do not allow original documents to be removed. That is the reason a copy was made."

"Please check again, there must be some mistake. Perhaps you overlooked it the first time."

"Mikaela."

I barely heard Brodie in my determination that it had to be there.

"I assure you, *madame*. The document is not there. It may perhaps be found at a later time. My apologies.

"If you would care to leave the copy with us, we will attempt to find the original document. If it cannot be found, at least there would be this record."

I refused to leave it with him. "I cannot. It is all we have."

"I understand. Perhaps in time it will be found, but we have very few people here ..."

There was more, but I didn't listen. And I knew it would do no good to argue with him. He apologized again as we left.

"I had hoped ..." I started to say something, as we then left the building. And in that way Brodie understood.

"I know."

"To come this far." The frustration was there, along with the anger. I held onto it as we walked to our hotel. And then a little longer as he went to the front desk for the key to our room.

"Is it possible that someone took it?" I asked as he returned. I could see that same thought in that dark gaze.

"Perhaps. Desperate people do desperate things."

"Victoria Grantham would have had a chance to do that before arriving in London."

"Aye."

I knew what he was doing, letting me *rattle on with my thoughts*, as he put it, in that way that I needed to make sense of things, turning my thoughts over and over in my head. He handed me the room key.

"I want to check with the telegraph clerk to see if there is a message."

And then he left me to those thoughts in that aggravating way that he also understood.

The concierge clerk directed me to the lift. I waited until it returned to the ground floor, then stepped inside and closed the gate. It made the slow climb to the third floor, then settled to a stop.

I stepped out onto the floor, glanced at the number on the room key, then made my way down the hall, still struggling with the failures of the day.

I found our room, and inserted the key into the lock.

There was no warning, nothing I saw or heard to warn me as I was slammed against the door. It opened, and I was sent sprawling to the floor of the room.

I attempted to roll, hindered by my skirt. I was grabbed by the collar of my coat, then viciously slapped. Light exploded in my head.

My attacker was experienced, it was impossible to escape, roll away, or bring a knee up as he bent over me. I drove the heel of my hand at his face and heard the sound as his nose was broken and blood splatted over the both of us.

He cursed, then raised his fist, fingers wrapped around the handle of a knife. The revolver in my bag was somewhere on the floor, and beyond reach. The moves I had learned to defend myself were impossible as he straddled me.

With both hands wrapped around his arm in an attempt to

stop him, it was clear that I was no match for his greater strength, certain I was about to feel the blade of that knife.

It was his scream I heard, not my own, and I was suddenly free of the weight that had pinned me as he was dragged backwards.

The sounds of struggle continued in the darkened room with only the light from the hallway that fell through the open door. There was sudden silence and then my attacker ran past and out the open door.

Brodie followed, briefly outlined in the light from the hall, then charged down the hallway. I scrambled cross the floor of the room, found my bag, pulled out the revolver, and aimed it toward the doorway.

"If ye fire the bloody thing, ye'll make yerself a widow."

I took a deep breath and a sound escaped, something very near a sob. I lowered the revolver as Brodie came across the room. And then another sound as he brought me to my feet.

His hands wrapped around my head, fingers digging into the tangled mess of my hair, that dark gaze boring into mine.

"Are ye all right?"

I nodded, then wrapped my arms around him, my face buried in the front of his jacket, as if I could melt into him, the warmth of his body as I began to shake ... and the blood!

"MOST WOMEN DON'T TAKE WELL to the sight of blood," Brodie commented as I carefully tugged at the sleeves of his jacket and laid it over the back of a chair in the room.

"I've had some experience," I replied. That brought a faint chuckle from him.

The door was closed. There hadn't been any inquiries from hotel staff about the sounds in the room. And for now, the man who had attacked me was gone.

Brodie shrugged out of his shirt with that bloodied sleeve. There was a smile on one corner of his mouth as he continued to watch me as I gently wiped away the blood on his lower arm. The cut wasn't deep, but it had bled nicely.

He reached up with his other hand, fingers lightly brushing my bruised cheek. It was there in the gentleness of his hand and the expression that appeared on his face, and in that dark gaze.

"Did ye get a look at the man?"

I had seen him twice before—the first time when I went to meet with Victoria Grantham. He had been waiting for her on the landing at the top of the stairs when our meeting abruptly ended. And then again at Dover. I had dismissed it at the time, but I was certain of it now.

"Aye, he followed us from London."

"Your arm needs to be bandaged."

He shook his head. "Some of that brandy will do." He gestured to the wide table near the hearth. "And a strip of cloth from yer underskirt."

"Will he come back?"

"He's more likely to find a place to hide and dress his own wound." That dark gaze held mine. "He hoped to find ye alone and be done with ye. He didna count on the fact that ye fight like a man, and it seems ye broke his nose. There was a lot of blood."

Including no doubt, the wound he had received.

"What if someone at the hotel notified the local police?"

He shook his head. "It's not likely. Or they would have been here already."

"There's no train to Calais until morning," I pointed out. I would have preferred to leave that night.

I looked around at the room—the furniture that had been overturned, and a good amount of blood on the carpet. No doubt from that broken nose.

"I'll find another room down the hall. There are not a lot of guests about. There is bound to be an empty one. That will go a long way to discourage any other visits should the man decide to return."

He stood as I finished bandaging his arm, then gently kissed me.

"Ye have a fine hand, lass. As long as there's not a revolver in it." He kissed me again.

"Prop the chair under the latch on the door."

He was only gone a few minutes.

Our new room was at the end of the hall by the stairway.

"I persuaded the guest to leave."

He was teasing of course.

"And bring the brandy."

We spent the night in that second room. Brodie went down to the restaurant as a bruise began to appear on my cheek which would undoubtedly have raised questions. He returned with roast chicken, vegetables, warm bread, and wine. However, there was no soup!

I slept fitfully, waking several times during the night at a sound from the hallway and found Brodie awake in the chair before the hearth.

"Go back to sleep," he said each time, and somehow I managed.

In the morning it seemed that he had been awake the entire night.

I had washed his shirt the night before and set it to dry in front of the hearth. He quickly dressed while I moved about a bit more slowly. Other than the cut on his arm, he appeared to have escaped relatively unscathed.

To say that I was sore in more places than my bruised cheek was a bit of an understatement. I hurt all over from being thrown against the door and then to the floor.

I made use of the adjoining washroom and set some order to my hair. When I stepped back into the room, we made a quick breakfast from the leftover baguette.

"It's cold and there is a bit of snow," he said, stepping away from the window.

He helped me with my coat and bag that contained the

copy of the document we'd brought with us, along with my notebook and the revolver, then wrapped his woolen scarf high around my neck so that it covered most of the bruise on my cheek.

"Aye, that will do."

We left the room.

At the concierge desk, he requested a driver to take us to the rail station. The same driver we had the day before arrived and we quickly climbed inside.

There was only a brief wait at the rail station for the morning train to Creil. Brodie purchased our fares. We quickly climbed aboard when the train arrived, both of us watchful for the man who had attacked me.

We didn't see him at the station or among the few passengers as we boarded. If he was going to return to London it seemed that it would be on another train.

Brodie purchased box lunches from a café at the station at Creil. The train that would take us to Calais arrived the next hour.

There were few people in the rail car for that return trip, as there were generally fewer travelers that time of year due to unpredictable weather.

We arrived in Calais the middle of the afternoon. There were no encounters on the trip there.

Brodie stepped down on the platform, then reached a hand to steady me. I stepped down as well and looked up into Munro's sharp blue gaze.

"Ye made the crossing well enough," Brodie commented.

"Aye, but there will be none the rest of the day with the storm that's come in."

I had dozed off on the trip from Creil and my thoughts were slow. Then there was only one. And the fear was there.

"Has something happened?" I asked. "Aunt Antonia? Lily?"

"They are safe," he replied. "Best to get out of the weather."

With no crossings the remainder of the day there was nothing for us to do but go to the inn where we'd stayed before and find a room for the night.

It was crowded with other travelers who were forced to stay over until the weather improved, as were other inns and a hotel, according to Munro.

Brodie was able to get one of the last rooms available. It seemed I would have to share the room with the two of them.

He had sent a telegram to London the night before and cautioned Munro about what had happened.

And in that way of having known each other for all those years, Munro had made arrangements with Mr. Brown, and then come to Calais.

I could only imagine my great aunt's response to Brown's men taking up temporary residence at Sussex Square. And then there was Lily.

"Her ladyship has the matter well in hand," Munro said of my great aunt. "The young miss as well, until I return."

And my sister?

"Safe," he replied. He looked at me as we sat at a table in the tavern on the main floor of the inn, and knowing me quite well, made only one comment.

"I hope ye gave as good as ye received."

Brodie explained what had happened.

"Aye, well the next time," Munro replied.

They both ordered ale, while I requested coffee.

We ate in the tavern. Several times, I noticed Brodie watching the door as someone arrived or departed.

Over ale and then supper he spoke quietly with Munro. He explained what we'd learned and what had happened at the hotel in Compiegne.

"What news do ye have?" Brodie asked him.

He had kept watch over the man Brodie had followed to Aldgate, and had made inquiries about him.

The man was German, according to what he was told. He learned a name—Kessler. Then made other inquiries. It seemed that Herr Kessler was a doctor.

"Not just any doctor, but a surgeon."

Why would Victoria Grantham have need of a doctor, more specifically a surgeon?

It made no sense, but as I had learned in our other inquiry cases, the clues we learned often made no sense until we uncovered that one piece of information that connected all of it, and everything came together.

There was more.

"The man is dead," Munro told us.

"How?" Brodie asked.

"At his shop when I returned. Someone had used his own instrument to kill him."

Which made it impossible to learn anything from the man.

I was exhausted, my cheek throbbed, and a headache had begun. I needed sleep.

Brodie stood as I rose from the chair at the table, and escorted me to our room. He helped me undress, then tucked me in bed with a thick comforter. His fingers brushed my cheek.

"We won't be long." The '*we,*' of course, included Munro.

"Munro?"

"Aye. He'll manage by the fire. I'll not have him in my bed. He snores."

I would have laughed, except that it hurt.

I caught his hand in mine as he stood to leave. The question was there ... a dozen questions were there. And no answers.

"We'll find out what the Grantham woman is about. What happened yesterday will have upset her plans. She will make a mistake and we'll be there to see it."

I nodded and curled into myself under the comforter.

I was only slightly aware when he returned to the room with Munro.

Brodie was not given to snoring, except if there was an abundance of whisky or ale. And then there was Munro.

While I had no practical experience in that regard, it did seem as if both men had indulged in a considerable amount of ale by the amount of noise I was surprised didn't rattle the walls of the room.

I buried my head, along with my bruised cheek, in the covers and somehow managed to go back to sleep.

There was a faint sliver of light beneath the shutters at the window when I finally conceded there would be no more sleep and slipped from the bed I shared with Brodie.

He moved into the spot I had occupied without waking, his snoring temporarily muffled with his face buried in the pillow.

I pulled a blanket from the bed, stepped carefully around the second snoring Scot under a heavy wool blanket in front of the hearth, then let myself out of the room and went down the hall to the loo.

When I returned, somewhat refreshed with soap and water,

I encountered a dark haired, dark eyed Scot in somewhat ill humor at the door to the room.

"Wot are ye about, lass, takin' herself off alone after what happened?" Brodie demanded.

There were still remnants of the headache from the day before. It was cold in the hallway, I was bare of foot, and in no mood to stand about in only my undergarments with only a blanket for warmth.

"I needed to use the room," I informed him. "It was not something that might wait for an escort, particularly two Scots who snore loud enough to wake the dead."

"What is all the noise?"

We both looked at Munro who appeared behind Brodie in the doorway, glowering at us.

There were moments when I was amazed by some small thing that completely flummoxed Brodie. This was one of those moments, as he stood there in just his trousers, bare of foot, with the bloodied bandage on one arm, a scowl on his face.

"I have no need of a guard when I need to use the loo!" I whispered quite vehemently, then stepped past the both of them as I returned to the room.

"There'll be no more sleep." Munro returned as well. He pulled on his boots then grabbed his jacket, and left the room.

Brodie found his shirt and pulled it on, then grabbed his boots.

"Ye canna go about in yer underthings as if it's of no matter, with another man about."

Another man? Munro?

He was quite disheveled as he tucked his shirt into his pants. And then there was the scowl. He scraped that mane of hair back. The scowl was still there.

"Munro has seen me dressed as a man, wounded with little more than what I am wearing now, and countless other times at Old Lodge in little more than my knickers before the morning fire."

He jerked one boot on then reached for the other.

"Aye," he snapped.

"What is this about, then?" I demanded. He yanked on his other boot, then stood.

He looked very much like some ancient Scot, ready to do battle.

"It isna so much about Munro," he finally said. "I trust him with my life, and yers. I know he would never have a thought about ye as a woman ... not in that way. Even tho' ye are most fetchin' in yer underthings," he admitted, as the scowl faded.

Fetching. Now there was a word to impress a woman.

"I suppose it's everything that happened in Compiegne," he attempted to explain. "I woke, and ye were gone ..."

"I had gone to the loo," I reminded him.

"Aye."

He reached out and laid his hand gently on my bruised cheek. The scowl was gone, replaced with another expression.

"Ah, Mikaela Forsythe, ye tear me heart out, with the way ye look at me, the way I need ye.

"When that man attacked ye, my only thought was that I might lose ye and there was somethin' near rage. Then, to find ye gone this mornin' ..."

I did understand—the pain of his childhood, the loss, then orphaned to the streets, and the years since.

"I know," I told him and meant it. "However, you do realize that it will happen again."

Those dark eyes narrowed, and the scowl returned.

It was really too tempting. I laid my hand over his.

"I will need to use the loo again."

With me in my knickers and a bruise on my cheek, he cursed ... then kissed me quite thoroughly.

Brodie's scarf was tucked high about my neck, more for warmth than any concern that someone might see the bruise on my cheek as we waited to board the steamer for the trip back across the channel. It also provided the opportunity to search the faces of our fellow passengers who gathered nearby.

Word had reached the inn that the steamer would make the crossing. To say that the weather was calmer than the day before seemed a bit optimistic, as whitecaps churned the waves that swirled about the dock.

Brodie left me with my 'protector' when we arrived, and made a walk about the dock as we waited to board, that dark gaze shielded beneath the bill of his cap as he moved among the other passengers huddled in the building and under the eaves.

"He is not here," he announced in a low voice when he returned.

I should have been relieved that the man who had attacked me was not there. Yet, that meant that he was still out there somewhere—and having escaped would he try again?

The day I met with Victoria Grantham, he had been at Grantham Manor, standing on the landing at the top of the stairs as I left.

Who was he? A servant? Companion? Lover?

He had followed us to Compiegne. And now the man Munro had been asked to follow was dead.

What did it have to do with Victoria Grantham's claim?

～

We made the train at Dover, then the return rail trip to London without further incident.

Brodie insisted that I go to the townhouse to rest, but I refused and accompanied him back to the office on the Strand.

Munro returned with us as far as the office, then continued on to Sussex Square.

Mr. Cavendish was there, as well as the hound. He frowned, obviously at the sight of the bruise, but made no comment on it.

"Good to see ye, miss."

Rupert insisted on accompanying us up the stairs to the office.

There was no fuss as we entered the office, none of the usual anticipation for food. He simply followed me to my desk, then curled on the floor at my feet, soulful eyes watching me.

"Worthless beast," Brodie said, not unkindly.

Good boy, I thought, with the usual scratch behind his ears.

Rupert made his usual response, a thump of his tail, then promptly went to sleep.

I took out my notebook, then went to the blackboard to add notes I had made on the trip from Dover.

Motive, means, opportunity.

The *'means'* and *'opportunity'* were obvious with that attack in Compiegne. But for what reason? What was the motive?

Victoria Grantham's claim, that she only wanted to know her real family? Financial gain? Surely getting hands on my great aunt's wealth could be a possible motive. It wouldn't be the first time that someone attempted that.

With what had happened in Compiegne, it seemed that it

was something far more. And now the man I had seen leaving the Grantham Manor was dead.

What was his part in all of this? Who had killed him? And for what reason?

The answer seemed obvious—Victoria Grantham.

Was she taking care of 'loose ends,' as Brodie called it?

It sounded preposterous. And yet ...

I glanced at the manuscript Victoria Grantham had written and then sent to my brother-in-law with the hope of having it published; that bore a striking resemblance to the details of my life, and her claim that she only wanted to know her family.

The thought was there even as I attempted to push it away. It was simply too bizarre, terrifying. And insane?

I thought of the encounters with Victoria Grantham—at the book shop, her appearance at the gallery the night of Linnie's art showing, then again at the German gymnasium.

Places and events that were part of *my* life!

And now the disappearance of that document from the records at Compiegne, that might prove that it was all a deception, followed by the attack that might have succeeded if Brodie had not been there.

It was there in the words I had added to that improbable list of clues, glaring back at me from the blackboard. The piece of chalk snapped in my fingers.

I came away from the board and the glaring possibility, and wrapped my arms around myself trying to understand, to comprehend what madness had driven Victoria Grantham to do such things.

I heard a small sound and realized I had made that sound, almost a whimper like a wounded animal.

I turned away from the chalkboard, unable to look at the words ... at the truth.

"Brodie …?"

I felt as if I couldn't breathe. Was that even my own voice?

He pulled me into his arms.

"I'm here, lass."

We sat in one of the overstuffed chairs in front of his desk for the longest time.

I had fought him at first. Fought the anger of that glaring truth, then fought the fear for my sister, my great aunt, Lily …

Impossible. I kept coming back to that word.

How could Victoria Grantham hope to make any of them accept her …?

I had tried to push Brodie away. He held on, and somewhere between the truth and the anger, he pulled me down into that chair and held me, as I cursed and wept, then curled against him until the rage was spent.

"What is to be done?" I asked.

The truth was that we had no evidence to prove any of it. With the physician's death and the disappearance of the man who had attacked me, there was no one who might be persuaded to expose Victoria Grantham's scheme. There was only Victoria Grantham.

I insisted on checking on both James and my sister, as well as my great aunt.

Only James had been aware of the men who discreetly followed him from home to office and then back again. My sister had been oblivious to it, as I had insisted in consideration of her condition.

However, my great aunt was another matter. I was reminded as we took a coach to Sussex Square that this was a woman who was descended from a ruthless king, had outlived several '*gentlemen friends,*' as she referred to them, and boldly traveled to Africa while other friends who were still alive were in their rocking chairs.

Adding to that, she motored fearlessly across London whenever she chose, amidst all sorts of persons on the streets who would not have hesitated to accost her, and had once chased drawn a man who had attempted it with a pistol—the apple had not fallen far from that tree.

And then there was Lily. I was determined to protect all of them.

I greeted Mr. Symons as we arrived. Munro was there as well, and informed us that my great aunt was in the drawing room.

I wasn't at all certain what to make of his expression in the look he gave Brodie.

"Here you are, dear," Aunt Antonia exclaimed. "Safe and sound, I see. Munro did share your encounter with us. You're in time to join us for the next hand."

It appeared to be a game of poker, of all things, as she shuffled a deck of cards and called for bets to be placed from those at the table, that included Lily, and Mr. Brown!

Thirteen

I MIGHT NOT HAVE RECOGNIZED him were it not for the man's thick stature, large paws for hands, and his gruff response as my great aunt called for bets. The sight of him at the gaming table with a polite demeanor was most unusual in contrast to his usually gruff manner.

Aunt Antonia promptly dealt a round of cards in a game that I recognized as poker. Lily looked at her cards, placed a bet, then called for one card. Mr. Brown inspected his cards, cursed, then threw down his entire hand and rose from the table.

"That is the third hand I've lost this morning to the woman!" he exclaimed by way of a greeting. "I know she cheats, but I haven't been able to determine just how."

He nodded at Brodie, then looked at me overlong with that sharp gaze that seemed to see everything.

I had made an attempt to hide the bruise with some powder before leaving the office so as not to alarm Aunt Antonia. I thought it quite successful, until now.

Brown motioned for Brodie to follow him and they left the parlor.

"It seems that you have had quite an adventure," Aunt Antonia commented with a frown, as she laid her cards on the table and gave several coins to Lily.

"Come along, dear," she said, as she rose from her chair. "Munro has spoken of your trip to Compiegne."

I followed her into the solar. Rain pelted the glass as she poured two glasses of whisky and handed one to me. "You must tell me everything," she said as Lily joined us. "That bruise is quite dreadful. I do hope that you gave as good as you received? And speak plainly, Mikaela. If there is a threat to the family, then I will hear all of it."

I explained what Brodie and I knew, what we had learned in Compiegne, the missing document that I had hoped might reveal the truth about Victoria Grantham's birth, then the attack on me.

"And Mr. Munro's part in this? He left quite suddenly and left us with Mr. Brown, although I can say that his presence has been most interesting."

I shared that Brodie had asked Munro to watch the man we had seen leaving Grantham Manor after my meeting with Victoria Grantham.

She waited expectantly.

"It appears that he was a physician, more specifically a surgeon."

"In Aldgate?" she remarked. "Somewhat unusual. And I assume he is dead. That, of course, explains Munro's sudden departure and the presence of Mr. Brown," she commented. "Hardly necessary, dear. Should there be any danger, we are well armed here at Sussex Square. Although I will admit, it has been most entertaining to have Mr. Brown with us. And what of Lenore and James?"

I explained that he and Brodie had also arranged for some of his men to discreetly provide protection for them.

In for a penny, in for a pound. I had shared this much, there was hardly any point in keeping anything from her.

I then shared about the manuscript that had been delivered to my brother-in-law.

"And she has written a novel?" She was thoughtful. "And that dreadful appearance of hers ... No criticism, dear. You are quite lovely, but there was something about the woman when we met at the gallery showing ... that seemed quite odd."

She had emptied her glass and poured more for herself. I declined.

"It does seem as if the woman is quite deranged. It is possible that her financial situation is part of it, but that is no excuse for the attack on you. I believe it's called 'attempted murder.'"

I would have laughed if the 'situation' wasn't so dangerous. I might have expected Aunt Antonia to be wearing a deerstalker hat with her determination to participate in one of our inquiry cases.

And then in that way that reminded me of myself, she continued on.

"One man is dead, another has disappeared in France, and you've been accosted. He will undoubtedly contact her," she added. "Which will only make her more determined to carry out her plan.

"The woman must be stopped!"

Brodie eventually returned, his expression no expression at all, one I was familiar with from past inquiry cases when he was deep in thought, which meant that he and Munro had thoroughly discussed the situation with Mr. Brown.

We were informed that Mr. Brown had departed—even

though no one had seen him leave, such was the man's ability to move about. Much like someone else, I knew. Yet, two of his men were to remain at Sussex Square.

"Do ye want me to accompany ye?" Munro asked when Brodie requested the use of my great aunt's coach and driver as we prepared to leave.

Brodie shook his head. "It's best ye remain here until this is over. I will send word if there is a need."

Lily stood quiet as a statue as we prepared to leave, then approached me.

"I won't let anyone hurt her," she said in a quiet but determined voice, the accent slipping through as it did with Brodie when he was angry.

She was no longer the girl I had brought from Scotland as my ward, but a very determined young woman.

I pressed my hand against her cheek.

"I'm relying on you."

The ride to the office was quiet, except for the sounds of the street beyond the coach. Yet I was aware that Brodie watched me from where he sat.

"Ye spoke with Lady Antonia?"

I nodded. "There was no reason not to tell her what had happened." I smiled.

"I feel sorry for anyone who attempts to harm her or Lily."

Still, I was most grateful that Munro and two of Mr. Brown's men were there.

His voice softened. "Aye, I believe the woman can be quite formidable."

We continued a distance in silence. There was something

that was there at the edge of my thoughts as I told my great aunt everything that had happened.

Until now, Victoria Grantham had the advantage in her insane plan. I was quite through with that.

She would not stop or go away. That was quite clear, and I was not willing to simply wait for whatever she might do when she learned her scheme in Compiegne had failed.

"Wot are ye thinkin', lass?" Brodie asked as he had so many times. He could never know how much that meant to me.

There was no argument against it. No angry attempt to convince me otherwise as we neared the Strand.

He listened.

"If anything should happen to Linnie, Aunt Antonia, or Lily ..." I continued. "I refuse to simply wait for what she might do next. You surely have experience with this from when you were with the MET."

Or possibly from that other life before he joined the MET.

"Do ye know what ye are saying?"

I did.

I was prepared to give Victoria Grantham what she wanted —myself. I had become a target in what we now believed was some insane plan to insert herself into our family no matter what it took, no matter the cost.

Everything she had done proved that she would not stop, not even at murder. I was not willing to let her succeed in that.

Brodie stared out the window of the coach. What did he see? Something, nothing, lost in thought. Perhaps thinking of a way to talk me out of it? He eventually turned back. That dark gaze met mine.

"Yer to do exactly as I say in this."

For once, I did not argue.

We remained at the office on the Strand that night, then rose early the next morning. I had slept fitfully, Brodie not at all, it appeared.

He set the coffee on the coal stove while I washed, found clean clothes in a drawer, and set some order to myself. He then poured us both a cup of coffee. It was strong and hot, just what I needed.

"Where do we begin?" I asked, holding my cup in both hands to warm them.

"It's safe to say that the woman knows about the man's failure in the attack in Compiegne," he pointed out. "He would only have needed to send a telegram.

"What with that manuscript she wrote, it's obvious that she knows a good many things about ye already. It's possible that she's followed ye for some time in her scheme."

I hadn't noticed anyone, and yet she had known to send her man after us when we left for France. I felt another cold chill.

Was she insane? What would she do next?

"We have to use that against her," he continued. "Follow where she goes, see, then not seen, so that she doesna know what to expect next." He paused.

"The woman is obviously not of sound mind. But she's clever and unpredictable ..."

"Therefore, I have to be clever and unpredictable," I replied the obvious.

He nodded. "It will be dangerous, particularly now when her first attempt on yer life failed."

I should have been afraid. I wasn't—there was too much at risk.

"The alternative would be to do nothing," I commented.

"And simply wait until she does something else. I won't take that chance."

"Aye," he said as he finished erasing the information on the board that I had so carefully written.

"You think that she would come here?"

"I believe that anything is possible when someone becomes desperate. I've seen it and experienced it."

I watched as he finished cleaning the board, set the felt eraser on the chalk rail very carefully, then turned and slowly came toward me

"Do ye know wot ye are askin' of me?" he asked. "To allow ye to deliberately put yerself in danger? If anything should happen to ye," he added, "ye should know that she will not live to see the inside of a court or a ward at Bedlam."

"It cannot be any worse than facing down Marie Nikola in our first inquiry case."

I had tried for some measure of humor. He was not amused.

"How are we to begin?" I asked.

"There is always someone who would know appointments she might have; places she would go. What of the housekeeper?"

"Ye said the woman appeared to want to tell ye somethin' that day as ye left after yer meetin' with Victoria Grantham."

"Perhaps, yet even if she is willing to tell us, it could be dangerous for her," I pointed out. "Why would she take the risk?"

"Perhaps to save herself. We need to know where the woman will be, and when."

"She answered the telephone when I called previously. I might be able to persuade her to meet with me."

"Aye. It is worth a try. But ye should be prepared that she will refuse to meet ye."

I did recognize that she might be suspicious, might refuse outright to meet with us. It was a chance I was willing to take, and carefully prepared what I would say. I then had the operator put through the call to Grantham Manor.

Mrs. Aldcott answered as she had previously. She did share that Victoria Grantham had left earlier for an appointment and was not expected until late. I then asked if she would be willing to meet with me about an important matter. A long silence followed.

She then questioned the reason. I relied on that previous brief exchange as I had left Grantham Manor.

"I believe that you know what it is about," I replied and then repeated my request to meet. "You tried to speak of it the day I was there."

She eventually agreed to meet at the office on the Strand and would leave right away.

It was a good hour's travel by coach from Waverly Place, and as it grew later, I became anxious.

What if Victoria Grantham had returned unexpectedly and questioned her? It could be dangerous for her.

What if Victoria Grantham came here, for one of those 'appointments' she told Mrs. Aldcott of?

What if ...?

The service bell rang and Brodie went to the landing. He returned with Mrs. Aldcott, who was obviously hesitant. Perhaps even afraid. And then she saw me.

"Forgive me, it's just that the resemblance is astonishing, even though I saw you before. And if she knew that I was here ... I have a little while before she returns."

"You're quite safe," I assured her and introduced Brodie.

He took her coat and the market basket she had brought with her, an excuse for her absence if she should be found out.

I invited her to sit in one of the overstuffed chairs. I sat across from her.

"We've just returned from France," I explained. "We were there in an attempt to learn more about Victoria Grantham's claim. You know of it?"

She nodded. "I saw the letter she had the solicitor write."

"There was an attempt on my life while we were there by the man I saw at the manor the day I met with her, and I have reason to believe that my family is in great danger with the claim she has made. I need your help to protect them."

She was hesitant and wary.

"Someone in your position would see things, the letter you mentioned, and perhaps other things." I continued. "Or you might overhear something. There was something you wanted to tell me that day. I need to know what that was."

She was still hesitant. "You must understand, I was with Sir Grantham and Lady Grantham for more than twenty years."

"And you do not wish to betray that loyalty." I understood. "But this isn't about your loyalty to them, it is about your mistress now, something that could end in tragedy."

For several moments I thought she might refuse to tell us more.

"I knew her as a child." She was still hesitant, as if struggling to find the right words.

"She was bright and curious. But something changed in her after she came home from school when Sir Grantham was very ill. There was a horrible argument with Lady Grantham."

She didn't know what it was about, but Victoria returned to school in France shortly afterward. When she finished school, she chose to remain in France except for only brief visits.

"All those years, Lady Grantham wrote to her, pleaded with her to come home. I posted the letters for her. There were only a few responses, that left the poor woman in tears. Then, several months ago, Miss Victoria returned. After all that time, and it was too late. Lady Grantham became ill shortly after and then passed."

Several months?

The solicitor who wrote to Sir Laughton stated that she had returned two months before.

And Lady Grantham became ill shortly after?

She shook her head. "She was not the girl I remembered—she had changed. She seemed preoccupied about something. She would be up all night, and more than once I heard her shouting to no one. She was angry. I thought it must be over the loss of her mother.

"That was when the doctor came."

"I saw a man leave that day I met with her."

She nodded. "She had a scar on her face from a childhood accident. It could hardly be seen, but she seemed to be obsessed with it. She said that he told her he could give her a new face.

"She left for an entire day, with no word. There were bandages when she returned. He came to the manor frequent after that, and they would close themselves off in the library."

That explained the smell of chloroform, to perhaps relieve the pain of the surgeries, and Mrs. Aldcott's description of spells.

Mr. Brimley spoke of possible side-effects. One of them was hallucinations.

"After some time, there didn't seem to be the need for him to return so often, only to change the bandages. She took the last ones off herself, and when I saw her ... I didn't recognize her."

"You should know the physician is dead," Brodie told her.

"Dead?" she replied with a stunned expression. "I never liked the man, but to think ..." She shook her head in disbelief.

"The poor man. I don't wish something like that for anyone." She looked at me as if trying to make sense of it.

"You believe that she did it?"

"Or someone killed him for her."

She shook her head. "She said there was no need for him any longer when I asked about him only a few days ago."

She was quiet for several moment, then looked up.

"It wasn't just the changes in her face, you know. It was something else, something frightening. I've never been a religious woman, you understand. But if there is evil in the world, it is inside her."

"There was another man on the stairway as I left that day, the same man who attacked me in Compiegne."

"René," she spat out with obvious dislike. "He arrived with her when she first returned. He does her bidding, and ... other things," she added. "He left three days ago." She glanced from me to Brodie.

"Do you believe that he killed the physician?"

"It's very possible," I replied. A loose end. "Has René returned?"

"If so, he's not been seen at the manor."

There was more.

"She wrote a book, what she called a novel, like the ones you write," she told us then. "She had purchased one of your books and she spent hours in the library with it. She said it was a way to learn how to write."

I exchanged a look with Brodie.

"But it's not just what she wrote, or her likeness to you," she tried to explain. "It's like I said, she's someone else." She shook her head.

"The way she talks, the things she says, as if she believes that she *is* you. I'm afraid what she will do."

"That is the reason we need your help."

I felt enormous sympathy for the poor woman. She had lost what had been her family for over twenty years.

"My poor mistress, Lady Anne. Better that she is gone and not aware what has happened." There were tears as she looked at me.

"I'll help you."

I EXPLAINED that I wanted to meet with Victoria, that we believed the attack at Compiegne was only part of what she intended.

"I have to protect my family," I told her.

I had thought a great deal about how it could be done, a meeting where Victoria Grantham thought she had the advantage.

"This is the only way to stop her."

"After what I have told you, you must not do this. She is not in her right mind. It is too dangerous!"

In the end I was able to convince her, and went to my desk to write a note to Victoria Grantham for when she returned to Grantham Manor.

"Tell her that it was brought by a courier," I explained.

In the note I asked for Victoria to meet me at three o'clock at Slater's tea room in Piccadilly, where prominent ladies of London went for afternoon tea. I had simply stated that we accepted her claim and wanted to welcome her to the family.

Brodie frowned when he read it. "Are ye certain about this?"

I wasn't certain about anything, yet it seemed logical that in the very least, Victoria Grantham would be intrigued to think that she had achieved what she wanted.

He handed the note back to me and I passed it to Mrs. Aldcott. She read it then tucked it into the small bag she carried.

I explained that she was to call the office when Victoria left for the meeting.

"You must realize that it would be dangerous for you to remain at Grantham Manor after this," I told her. "Is there some place you can go?"

She nodded. "My son has a shop in Harrow. I can go there."

"Do ye have the means?" Brodie inquired.

"Lady Anne saw that I was paid well enough, poor woman, and I've saved a good amount over the years."

She stood to leave. I accompanied her to the bottom of the stairs. Mr. Cavendish waved down a cab.

She turned as the driver arrived. "There is a difference, you see," she told me. She reached out and touched my cheek.

"Something very different that surgeon wasn't able to make the same." She stepped into the cab.

"Be careful," she said.

"And you as well," I told her.

Now, all we could do was wait.

We were taking a chance, to be certain. We had no way of knowing when she might call to tell us that she had given the note to Victoria Grantham, or even that Victoria would meet with me.

Mrs. Aldcott had described Victoria as intelligent and

clever. What if she saw through the deception? That could be dangerous for the poor woman.

Brodie made a telephone call to Munro at Sussex Square to tell him what we had planned, and we continued to wait as the noon hour came and went.

The telephone rang just past one o'clock, the shrill sound sharp in the silence of the office. Brodie answered the telephone then handed me the earpiece.

Victoria had returned and Mrs. Aldcott had given her the note.

"I was afraid she might be suspicious," she told me. "A strange look came over her. She changed her clothes, a gown that looks like the one you wore that other day. Then she told me there was no need to prepare supper and left."

She had waited to make certain Victoria didn't return before making that telephone call.

I thanked her, and reminded her that she could not remain at the manor.

"I've already packed my bag. I'll leave after we've spoken." There was a pause. "Take care, miss."

The call ended.

I glanced at the clock again, then at Brodie.

The gloom of the afternoon only added to my uneasiness as we left the office on the Strand for that meeting with Victoria Grantham.

Yet, in spite of the weather, or perhaps because of it, the store was quite crowded, and well-known ladies of London had gathered for afternoon tea.

I had picked Slater's for the meeting place at Brodie's insistence that it had to be a public place and one where he would be able to be present but not seen. In spite of the fact that the clientele at the tea room was mostly ladies, the store on the main floor brimmed with afternoon shoppers, and the stairway provided a means to be hidden and yet have access to the Tea Room.

There was more to the choice that I had not discussed with him. It was where I had gone in the past to meet with Linnie and my great aunt.

Was Victoria Grantham aware of that, had perhaps followed me there in the past?

There was no way to know for certain, yet it appeared that she had agreed to meet there. And she had chosen a gown similar to the one I had worn that previous day?

It was a chilling thought as I remembered something else Mrs. Aldcott had said, the way that Victoria Grantham spoke, things she said, as if she were me.

We arrived early ahead of the meeting time outside Slater's and I stepped down from the cab.

Brodie sent the cab man on his way as I entered the store alone in the event Victoria had already arrived. He was then to return after leaving the cab and enter the main floor of the store as I waited for her to arrive at the appointed time.

I informed the waitstaff that I was meeting someone there for tea, and was shown to a table very near the stairs.

I had been in dangerous situations before in our inquiry cases, yet not with so much at risk, considering what we knew now about Victoria Grantham.

In those other instances, I felt sure of myself with a certain confidence and determination.

It would have been a lie to say that I felt confident now. Still, I managed a polite smile as the waiter brought tea service with a plate of scones while I watched and waited.

Three o'clock came, then went as I continued to wait. Then four o'clock, with most of the ladies at other tables departed. The waiter brought me a note.

He'd been given instructions earlier to deliver it to me at precisely that time. I opened it.

So very sorry to have missed you. Perhaps another time at Sussex Square.

Lady Forsythe.

I stared at the note and read it again. It was polite, something that I might have written ... And the last part, *at Sussex Square?* An invitation?

In that moment I knew for certain Victoria Grantham would not be meeting me at Slater's. Yet, I did know where she had gone.

I stood suddenly, then ran for the stairs, oblivious to everything as I reached the store on the main floor.

"What is it?" Brodie demanded as he reached me.

I showed him the note. "She's gone to Sussex Square!"

I ran to find a driver.

People on the sidewalk who passed by stared at us as Brodie caught up with me on the sidewalk and stopped me.

"Wait!"

I tried to pull my arm free.

"She knows wot ye will do! It is what she wants, what this is about, for ye to go there so that she can finish this!"

"You don't understand ..." I argued.

"I *do* understand! And I know ye are smarter than to give her what she wants!"

I was terrified for Aunt Antonia, Lily, and everyone at Sussex Square—*my* family, not hers!

"Think! We dinna know if the man René, and perhaps others, might be with her! She wants ye to go there. It was the purpose of the note. Dinna give her what she wants!"

They were his family as well now, and I knew that he was right in what he was saying.

"Brodie ...?"

"I know, trust me."

The office was not far. He persuaded me to return with him so that we could decide what was to be done now.

There were those whom he could call on, possibly those at the agency, and then there was Mr. Brown with his organization, two of his men at Sussex Square from what we last knew. Along with my great aunt, Lily, Munro, and the household servants.

Victoria Grantham had been very clever. I needed to be more so.

When we arrived at the office, Brodie sent Mr. Cavendish off to find Mr. Brown. I ran up the steps to the office.

"Make a telephone call to yer brother-in-law. Tell him what has happened, so that Brown's men there will be on the watch for anyone who approaches their home.

"Then I want ye to draw a diagram of Sussex Square, every entrance including the servants' quarters, where deliveries are made, and the distance from the gate to the steps at the front."

I thought he must be mad.

"I'm not good at diagrams!" I fairly shouted at him.

"I know, it just needs to be good enough to recognize. We have to get inside without being seen."

When I started to protest that there wasn't time, he crossed from his desk where he had laid another revolver, and took hold of me by the shoulders.

"She may think that ye are the same, but she doesna know the place as ye do. That can make the difference if we get inside or no. Make the diagram."

I knew that he was right in this. Even if Victoria Grantham's scheme went back all those months before and she had ridden past Sussex Square as part of it, she didn't know it as I did. I had explored and crawled over most of it as a child, including the hidden rooms and passages of the oldest part of it.

I opened my notebook, found a blank page, and began to draw, as Brodie placed another telephone call to a man he had worked with at the MET but was now retired.

"Aye," Brodie said. "It's not a matter for the Metropolitan, not with some of the things had have gone down since I left. I need to know whom I can trust."

There was additional conversation, quite brief, then Brodie ended the call.

"Mr. Conner?" I asked.

Brodie nodded. "He knows a good many others like himself who can be called on. He can have his people watch the front gate after we arrive."

"You know what Mrs. Aldcott told us," I replied. "Victoria Grantham is quite mad. Do you believe that she might have already ...?" What I started to ask was there, but I couldn't say it.

He came to me then as he had when Victoria Grantham first made her claim, and took me in his arms.

"I believe that her ladyship is strong and bold like yerself, though she often plays much different. I've had some experience with that. Munro would give his life for what she has given him, and the girl is street-smart and not easily fooled.

"For all the woman believes that she *is* you, with her fine gowns and a new face, she is not, and she does not know you, or them. And I would wager on all of ye over her."

Of course he would say such things, yet I knew that it was true.

I held onto that as I finished the diagram, then folded it and put it into my bag. Along with the revolver, a hand-held lantern, and the knife Munro had given me a long time ago when I went off on my first adventure.

I then changed into clothes that Victoria Grantham would not recognize— trousers, shirt, and jacket, with boots and a cap I had worn in the past when setting off on one of our inquiry cases.

Mr. Cavendish was forced to leave a message for Mr. Brown with no assurance that he would receive it in time to assist us, but Brodie refused to wait any longer.

It was already dark over the streets of London as we set off in a rental coach, with no way of knowing what we would find at Sussex Square when we arrived.

Brodie had the driver follow the usual route we took when traveling to the fortress as he called it.

"I'm convinced the bloody place could take cannon fire and still be standing," he had described it.

I hadn't bothered to point out that it had, several hundred years earlier, with most of that part rebuilt.

"I canna imagine wot her Ladyship does there—it's large enough for an army under siege."

It had been a military fortress at one time after it was built by the King, one of my illustrious forebears by way of my great aunt. It was a marvelous place for a girl to disappear from her lessons and not be seen for several hours.

The 'Fortress' sprawled across an equally impressive tract of land that rivaled Hyde Park in size, and included an ancient forest, gardens, a stream, and now a car track. Along with stables and the coach barn.

As we drew near, I had Brodie stop the cab.

"Wot is it?"

The night fast approached, cold and wet with the drizzle of rain over all. Streetlamps were wrapped in halos of light as I had seen them dozens of times before, and lights glowed in the distance at Sussex Square.

It was true, Victoria Grantham was intelligent and clever. She had played this perfectly in drawing me away as she came here. And that note.

She knew that I would follow and had sent the note once she was inside the residence. Brodie was correct—she didn't truly know me.

She would be waiting and it was possible the man René would be with her. Mr. Conner and the men who came with him would eventually appear, yet we had no way of knowing if Mr. Brown would arrive in time.

Then the question—should we wait? And with it all, Victoria Grantham would be waiting.

Were those inside dead, as I feared from the beginning? Or was she playing some horrible game?

I needed to believe that we had the time needed to get inside, and stop her madness.

As a child, I had played out the stories my great aunt told me of our ancestors. It was possible, as Brodie thought, that the apple hadn't fallen far from that tree either.

"There's another entrance. It's somewhat longer to get there, but neither Victoria Grantham, nor anyone she has with her, will know of it."

"How far?"

I gave the driver instructions to follow the long road past the entrance, then the road north just before the river bridge that ran along a high street and bordered several old estates that had once been part of Sussex Square until they were sold in some sort of land transaction three or four hundred years earlier.

There were lights in the distance from two of the estates, while two more were hidden in the darkness that spread to the river, with dense foliage that we followed at the near side of the road.

While it had been some time since I had been there with Munro, I remembered the tree that seemed to hang suspended over the road as we had passed this way. Barren of leaves with the coming winter, I was able to find it, branches hanging over the road like the massive arms of the mythical forest creatures I had imagined as a child when off exploring.

I asked the driver to stop and stepped down from the cab. Less than a half-dozen yards ahead, I found what I was looking for.

Brodie had left the cab as well. The beam from his hand-held lantern played across the narrow dirt pathway, and the stones at the bottom of the wall.

"It's called the Smuggler's Gate. Once inside, there's a path through the forest that eventually reaches the stables and barn. Munro showed it to me."

"Smugglers?"

"It seems there were a great many of them about London in the past, and pirates, according to Aunt Antonia. It's always been a very active port. It's the reason the King had Sussex Square built."

"Yer ancestors. I dinna know one of mine."

I smiled in spite of everything. Smugglers, a pirate or two, and a Scot. It seemed appropriate.

He dismissed the driver, then returned.

"The gate is locked from the inside. The key is in the stables. You'll need to give me a leg up."

I grabbed onto a stone that protruded from the wall, then found a toe-hold, and pulled myself up the rest of the way. Brodie followed, easily reaching the top of the wall. He dropped down in the thick cover of branches, gorse, and juniper. Then reached up and caught me as I swung my legs over.

"How far?"

I found the pathway. "No more than a half mile."

We set off.

The way was often blocked by overgrowth or fallen limbs. We worked our way around, found the path once more, and continued until the shape of the coach barn loomed up out of the darkness.

We crossed the automobile track, and approached the gardens at the back of the manor.

This would most usually have been where Brodie told me to wait for him. He did not.

"The servant's entrance," he said in a lowered voice. I laid a hand on his arm.

The manor was well lit with electric there. We could be easily seen by Victoria Grantham or René if he was with her.

"The chapel."

"There's a chapel?"

I nodded and moved past the gardens into the older part of

Sussex Square where there was no electric, ten-foot-thick walls, the old granary, several storerooms, what my great aunt once told us was an old dungeon, and the chapel.

It was time-consuming as we moved through shadows, then along high stone walls of a tower, without light. We dared not turn on the hand-held lantern at risk that the beam of light might be seen.

At the other side of the chapel was the long passage that led to the medieval hall that connected to the new part of Sussex Square.

Exploring it no doubt fed my fascination with other places and my early adventures.

We eventually reached the chapel, crossed the medieval hall with the use of the lanterns, and reached an iron-framed oak door with a stout bar across.

Brodie lifted it with some effort. The door made a grating sound of old wood across the stone floor as he leaned into it, and we heard the faint sound of ... music.

Fifteen

"THE PIANO?" Brodie whispered.

I shook my head. That sound didn't come from the piano in the front parlor. It came from the solar. It was the gramophone.

Aunt Antonia had acquired it several months earlier. Lily had been quite taken with it. But was why was it playing?

When I started to step out into the main hall, Brodie pulled me back as one of my great aunt's servants passed by holding a tray with a crystal decanter and glasses.

The maid looked terrified as she continued on down the hall, then entered the solar. Here was a faint response, a brief silence, then the music began once more.

Where was the footman, Cook, the other servants, Mr. Symons? And the two men Mr. Brown had sent?

More important, where were my great aunt and Lily? Where was Munro?

The music ended, then began again, playing over and over. It was a German piece I recognized from an opera Lily had become fascinated with. Her only prior experience with music had been somewhat colorful tunes she had learned in a whore-house in Edinburgh.

The maid, a young woman by the name of Tilly, suddenly returned. She moved quickly as if trying to escape.

Brodie stepped into her path and grabbed her with one hand clamped over her mouth to prevent her crying out and alarming others. He pulled her back into the shadows along the wall.

Her eyes were saucers, then widened even further when she saw me. Brodie slowly lowered his hand.

"What has happened?"

"A woman and some men came here. They have weapons. There was a skirmish …"

"Where are Lady Montgomery and Miss Lily?" I whispered.

"Milady is there. They forced her to sit and then bound her."

"Is she all right?"

She nodded. "As near I can tell. The woman is in there as well, with Mr. Symons and some of the other servants."

"Where is Lily?"

"I don't rightly know, Miss Mikaela. When they burst in, she was upstairs in the Sword Room."

"Is anyone injured?"

One of the men struck Mr. Hastings when he came from the stables to see what was the matter. There was a lot of blood, but I think he's all right."

"There were men sent here earlier by Mr. Brown. Where are they now? And where is Munro?"

"I don't know. It all happened so fast, and the woman … I don't know! And that woman is in there. Oh, miss, it's frightening. I never seen anything like it …"

"How many men were with the woman?"

"Three, maybe four. It happened so fast. They came in through the main entrance. Mr. Symons tried to stop them. I seen him fall. He's still out there, poor man."

"Where were you goin' just now?" Brodie asked her.

"Back to the kitchen. One of the men is there, says he will kill anyone who attempts to leave. I've got to get back before they think I've run off."

One man. And it appeared that Victoria Grantham was in the solar.

"Is there anyone with the woman in the Solar?"

She nodded. "One of the men that came with her. One of the other girls said he must be French by his accent."

"René?" I whispered.

Brodie nodded. "Most likely."

"I gotta get back to the kitchen, miss. I don't want no one hurt on my account."

I didn't want her to go back. Trouble was, I didn't know where she might be safe. The other men who had apparently arrived with Victoria Grantham might be anywhere.

"Don't tell anyone that you've seen us."

"I won't, miss. But you got to help her ladyship." She looked back over her shoulder as she left, very near running toward the kitchens.

I looked at Brodie. Any moment we might be discovered. And neither Brown and his men, nor Mr. Conner had yet arrived.

"What are we to do?"

~

"Wot are ye about, girl!" Munro snapped as Lily bent over him from where she knelt on the floor of the wine cellar.

"I'm trying to keep you from bleeding to death!" she snapped as she tore another strip of cloth from the skirt of her gown.

Beside her lay the flintlock pistol she'd had in her hand when Munro dragged her from the second-floor sword room.

Munro listened now for any sounds that might tell him what was happening, but the wine cellar filled with casks of both wine and whisky was several feet below the main floor, and each of those feet in the place was made of cut stone.

One of Brown's men was dead. He saw the body as he went to the second floor by way of the servants' stairs to find the girl. She had met him at the door with the damn pistol.

He'd grabbed her and dragged her down those stairs, then past the servants' quarters toward the cellar.

There were screams from the women as everyone ran about in panic, and he'd thought of her ladyship.

Where was she? Had she been abducted?

Brodie had called and warned them. Brown was to send more men, but they hadn't arrived.

He cursed as the chit tightened the bandage she'd ripped from the skirt of her gown and then wrapped around his leg.

The man had come at them as he pulled her toward the cellar doors. If he'd been alone the outcome might have been different, but he'd protected the girl and paid for it.

The man caught him at the stairs that led down into the cellar. He only had time to push her ahead the rest of the way down, then took the blow across his upper leg.

There wasn't a second blow from the man, as he felt the blood stream down his leg and nearly fell the rest of the way. And she was there, no bigger than a minute, hitching her shoulder under his arm as if she could take his weight off his leg.

And she had.

She was strong. She'd been up there in that room, swinging those swords about and practicing the moves Miss Mikaela showed her, as if she had something to prove to someone. Or perhaps herself?

She loosened the cloth now around his leg, waited, then slowly tightened it again.

"Wot the devil are ye doin? Leave it be, girl. There's more important things to do. I need to find her ladyship."

She sat back on her heels and glared at him in the light from the single lamp on the wall. In that sputtering light, she looked like some fierce creature sprung from shadows—formidable, even if she was a pretty thing. She would bedevil some man one day.

"I'm tempted to leave it as is. But if I do, then you will have to learn to wheel yerself about like Mr. Cavendish at Mr. Brodie's office, for you will surely bleed to death or lose the leg!

"And if you have a thought of trying to climb those stairs, I'll knock yer other leg from under you. And I can do it." She tightened the bandage again.

He glared back at her. "We need to know what has happened. Where everyone is. Who's injured?"

"Aye," she replied in a quiet voice. "I'll go."

"The devil ye will."

"The devil I won't," she said, then told him, "Loosen it and leave it for a few minutes, then tighten it again."

And she was gone.

Munro cursed himself, and the wound at his leg. Then cursed her foolishness as he pushed to his feet. He reached the stairs and slowly climbed back to the top.

~

I looked at Brodie as the music from the gramophone played once more, that same piece over and over.

Neither Mr. Conner nor Mr. Brown and their men had arrived.

"We must do something," I told Brodie. "The woman is insane. She might kill her."

There was only one thing I could think of that might stop Victoria Grantham, even if it was for only a few minutes.

"I want to go in there." I saw the objection in the expression on his face.

"You know it's the only way, and it will give you time."

"Mikaela ..." He didn't say the rest of it.

"It's the reason we came here. Our family is here. They're in danger."

He slowly nodded. "Ye have the revolver?"

I nodded.

"When ye enter the room don't take the time to look for yer great aunt. Ye must look for those that have her and the others, scan the room, find them. There is no way of knowing what the Grantham woman and her cohorts will do."

I nodded. He was right. I had said it myself that she was insane.

"Ye'll not go in there alone. I'll be there with ye, but dinna look for me. I'll be going for the man, René. The girl said he was there as well."

I nodded again. I trusted him. The only other objective, I thought, was not to get ourselves killed.

"Check the revolver."

I checked it. I expected my hands to be shaking. They weren't.

He kissed me then. "Go, before that cursed music stops again, and do as I said."

I stepped out of the shadows along the wall, looked for anyone else about, then quickly made my way to the entrance to the solar. I caught a brief movement and knew Brodie was there, only a few paces behind.

The steel revolver was cool beneath my hand in my pocket as I entered the solar, and stared at the bizarre, grotesque scene as the music played.

Victoria Grantham danced in the middle of the room, her red gown much like the one I had worn, reflected in the glass panes in the walls. Around and around, she whirled to the music, laughing she danced about the room.

Anything I imagined could not have prepared me for the hideous spectacle before me.

It was like watching myself—my face, my hair ... me! Only it wasn't me, but a pathetic version as she continued to dance and pirouette around the room, her eyes bright with the madness that had brought us all here.

And the man who had attacked me was there, watching her.

He didn't see me. She didn't see me as I slipped behind the handful of servants who stood there, forced to watch the madness, and a glimpse of my great aunt, defiant, bound to her chair. Then I stopped the music, stopped the madness.

Victoria Grantham spun around as the music died

She stared at me. "I knew you would accept my invitation. I knew you would come. I've watched you all these months, but I waited ... to claim what is mine. What was always mine.

"Do you understand?" she shrieked. "My name, mine! Not a secret kept hidden until I found those letters. And the other papers that prove who I am! Lady Forsythe.

"Look at them." She made a sweeping gesture about the room. "They know who I am. Look at me! Tell me what you see!" she screamed as she came at me.

"Tell me!"

I saw the knife in her hand as the man who attacked me in Compiegne lunged toward my great aunt. And Brodie was there.

As Victoria Grantham came at me, screaming with rage and whatever demons possessed her, I looked into that face so like mine ... but not mine. Her hair wild about her head and shoulders, so like mine ... but not.

She screamed and came at me. I swept her feet from under her. She pushed to her feet, then came at me once more, her hands like claws.

A single shot cracked sharply. Smoke filled the air.

Lily stood at the entrance to the room, a fierce expression on her face, and a flintlock pistol in her hand.

The nightmare was over.

Epilogue

MY FAMILY WAS SAFE.

There were wounds and bruises of course from that horrible night, but they would heal. Even Munro, in spite of himself. Bloody, stubborn Scot.

Mr. Brown had lost three of his men in what I was certain evened the number of favors between him and Brodie.

Mr. Conner had arrived as well that night, though somewhat delayed, saw the situation well in hand, and had promptly left for the nearest tavern. Another stubborn Scot.

Three men that Victoria Grantham had hired had been killed that night, either by Mr. Brown's men or possibly Brodie, but he admitted nothing in the matter.

The man, René, lover, co-conspirator, murderer, and Victoria Grantham herself, along with the madness that had driven her, were both dead.

I had looked down at her that night, eyes wide, staring, but seeing nothing, with the damage from the surgeries she had sought to look like me, the marled features, skin curled back where it had separated at an incision that hadn't fully healed, her mouth gaping open.

Brodie said the memory of it would fade in time. I wasn't certain that I believed that.

Of course, the newspapers had a field day with the story, including Theodolphus Burke. He had somewhat redeemed himself with his publisher by mentioning that he had contributed to solving the case. My opinion of him had not changed.

Aunt Antonia's lawyer, Sir Laughton, had Victoria Grantland's claim dismissed 'post mortem,' after death, a mere formality so there could be no future claims made against my great aunt's estate.

As for my great aunt, she had suffered no lasting ill effects from the ordeal. As she had informed everyone, "I have experienced far more serious situations, yet I can always count on Brodie." After all, he was a man who could be trusted.

"What about the housekeeper?" Brodie had asked afterward.

"I met with her before she left to join her son and his wife after the Grantham residence was closed. She is still grieving the loss of her employer. They were quite close. She's convinced that she had been murdered by her daughter."

Possibly narcotics? I thought.

Surely the timing was suspicious, but there was no one left to pursue the possibility on her behalf.

I had accompanied Mrs. Aldcott to Highgate Cemetery to place flowers on Anne Grantham's grave.

As we were leaving, we encountered a man I recognized as Sir George Trevelyan, who had been acquainted with my father, one of his club gaming partners. I did wonder what

Lady Trevelyan might have known that she had refused to discuss.

As for that lost document that had conveniently disappeared from the Town Hall records at Compiegne? The truth was, without that document, there was no way to prove who Victoria Grantham's father was.

And then there was Lily.

She was very different now from the girl I had brought from Edinburgh as my ward. We had all known that it would happen. But that night at Sussex Square, when I saw her at the entrance to the solar with that pistol in her hand, I knew the young girl was no more. She had been replaced by a strong-willed, intelligent young woman with a will of her own.

The dust had settled the past month. My sister and her husband were well into Christmas holiday plans, while Aunt Antonia had undertaken the decoration of a new nursery at Sussex Square in anticipation of the arrival of a member of the next generation of Montgomery offspring.

As for those letters that my father had written to Anne Grantham ...

"What will ye do with them?" Brodie asked, surrounded by the pleasant aroma of pipe smoke as we sat before the fire in the hearth at the office on the Strand.

"I read them again," I replied.

I could keep them, a sort of memento.

But a memento of what? Of whom?

Someone I had barely known, whose secrets and failings had caused so much pain for my mother and haunted me for too long. Like a ghost of the past?

But there was nothing there, nothing that meant anything to me.

I tossed them onto the fire in the hearth, and watched them burn.

Author Note

Just a few words about *Deadly Ghost...*

We all have ghosts from the past—experiences both good and bad, the things that live with us.

Such was the case for Mikaela. It's been a deeply emotional journey for her. Her ghost of the past was that horrific day as a child when she discovered her father dead. And now secrets that she is forced to confront with the woman who had come forward and made that devastating claim.

Mikaela has carried that with her, along with more than a little anger, and those painful memories, just as Brodie was forced to confront his past in *A Deadly Vow*. Who better to understand than the man who shares her life?

As with the other books in the Deadly Series, there were many innovations and inventions of the late 19th century, with some far earlier.

Insanity was nothing new in the 19th century, it simply had a new name. It was called lunacy or melancholia in the 1800's, and there were many insane asylums, including the notorious

Bedlam, which is mentioned, where women were sent for behaving in ways the male-dominated societies did not agree with.

The symptoms mentioned were often brought on by hallucinogenics found in narcotics that were outlawed at the time except for medicinal use, yet still found their way throughout English Society. Chloroform, and along with that, arsenic was readily available at any marketplace.

Plastic surgery is an ancient practice from the time of the Pharaohs of Egypt according to sources, right along with brain and other complicated surgeries. They were quite advanced. For the sake of the story, I used the complications that can arise for some. It worked for the story and the ending that Mikaela faces.

Hair dye was common by the end of the 19th century, with dyes made from natural plants, and included henna, the red in the woman's hair to add to her scheme of turning herself into Mikaela (see brief about psychosis above). Victoria's psychosis was triggered by the lie about who her real father was that she used against Mikaela.

The case I had them working in the beginning was a way of showing that these two very intelligent, competent people work well together, and on their own as well. And it does hook Brodie back into the Agency, along with Mikaela.

The mention of 'side-eye' was too good to pass up. It is nothing new, mentioned as early as 1797. And of course it had to be with Lily.

Homes for women who needed a place to go to have their unborn child were common, particularly if it was in another country where it could be kept secret.

The goggles which Aunt Antonia wears when motoring

about and terrorizing the people on the streets of London have been used since the 14th century for a variety of reasons.

The use of citric acid—lemon juice—to both hide and reveal hidden messages with heat, came into use during WWI. I took the liberty of moving it earlier for the sake of the story, and to foreshadow future storylines.

Water towers for producing water were quite common among those with property. The flow of water turned a turbine that generated electricity. Of course, Lady Antonia would insist on having one to avoid those pesky electric outages.

As for the gramophone in the end chapters, it was invented in 1887, with a stylus that read vibrations on a grooved disk or cylinder, no electricity required as the cylinder or disc was driven by a spring-driven motor.

I am so very grateful for each and every one of you who share these adventures with Brodie and Mikaela, Munro, and other characters, including Lily. As Mikaela has observed, she is no longer a girl but a young woman, and very much like herself, with adventures that will challenge them all in forthcoming stories.

Clan Fraser

Betrayed

Revenge

Outlaws, Scoundrels & Lawmen

Desperado's Caress

Passion's Splendor

Silver Mistress

Memory and Desire

Desire's Flame

Silken Surrender

Angels, Devils, Rebels & Rogues

Ravished

Always My Love

Seductive Caress

Seduced

Deceived

"I want to write a book ..." she said.

"Then do it," he said.

And she did, and received two offers for that first book proposal.

A dozen historical romances later, and a prophecy from a gifted psychic and the Legacy Series was created, expanding to seven additional titles.

Along the way, two film options, and numerous book awards.

But wait, there's more a voice whispered, after a trip to Scotland and a visit to the standing stones in the far north, and as old as Stonehenge, sign posts the voice told her, and the Clan Fraser books that have followed that told the beginnings of the clan and the family she was part of ...

And now ... murder and mystery set against the backdrop of Victorian London in the new Angus Brodie and Mikaela Forsythe series, with an assortment of conspirators and murderers in the brave new world after the Industrial Revolution where terrorists threaten and the world spins closer to war.

When she is not exploring the Darkness of the fantasy world, or pursuing ancestors in ancient Scotland, she lives in the mountains near Yosemite National Park with bears and mountain lions, and plots murder and revenge.

And did I mention fierce, beautiful women and dangerous, handsome men?

They're there, waiting ...

Join Carla's Newsletter